G

TEN WAY STREET

Whether in her serious literary novels, her children's books, or the lighter romances written under the pseudonym Susan Scarlett, Noel Streatfeild wrote about what she knew, and put to good use the experiences of her early home life and career. So from her vicarage upbringing we have *Parson's Nine*, *Under the Rainbow*, *Peter and Paul* and *The Bell Family.* From her work in munitions at the Woolwich Arsenal in World War I we gain *Murder While You Work.* From her social work in Deptford came *Tops and Bottoms,* and her extensive war work in Civil Defence and the WVS went into *I Ordered a Table for Six, Saplings* and *When the Siren Wailed.* There was even a short spell of modelling which she used in *Clothes-Pegs* and *Peter and Paul.* And then there was the theatre, where her ten year acting career embraced many branches of the profession. Chorus girls and concert parties (*It Pays to be Good, Poppies for England*), pantomime, with its troupe of children, (*Wintle's Wonders*), ballet training (*Ballet Shoes, Pirouette*), a touring Shakespeare company and her eventual disillusionment with the profession (*The Whicharts*) - all of these found their way into her books. She had a long and distinguished literary career with 90 books, the Carnegie Medal and an O.B.E. to her credit.

TEN WAY STREET

SUSAN SCARLETT

Greyladies

Published by
Greyladies
an imprint of The Old Children's Bookshelf
175 Canongate, Edinburgh EH8 8BN

© Noel Streatfeild 1940
This edition first published 2012
Design and layout © Shirley Neilson 2012
Cover image © Mary Evans / The Estate of Charles
Robinson™/ Pollinger Limited

ISBN   978-1-907503-18-4

Set in Sylfaen / Perpetua
Printed and bound by the MPG Books Group,
Bodmin and Kings Lynn.

TEN WAY STREET

CHAPTER ONE

BEVERLEY SHAW pulled the collar of her cheap brown overcoat up to her eyes, and tucked her arm through her friend Sarah's.

"Ugh, it's cold when you get outside. They keep cinemas so snug, it makes the street seem worse."

"It was a good picture," said Sarah. "I do like Jean Arthur, she's more like us than most film stars."

Beverley gave Sarah's arm a squeeze.

"It was nice of you to take me. I'll take you when I've got a job." She looked at her watch. "It's quite early, will you come back to the hostel and have a hot drink?" Sarah nodded. "How's things?"

Sarah sighed.

"Well of course they're awful. I never knew that parsons could be so poor. I mean I thought they always had plenty to eat and all that sort of thing. I'm not very expensive as governesses go, but sometimes I'm ashamed to take the money."

"How's Mrs. Elton?"

"Dreadfully bad. Of course it's a miracle she's alive at all. It's awfully hard on Mr. Elton; vicarages do need a wife who can get about. I do what I can to help, but of course with three children to look after, I don't get much time."

Beverley stopped, they were under a lamp-post. Her red curls under her hat glowed, her face was alight with eagerness.

"Oh, goodness, I hope I get a job like that. Somewhere where I'm really needed. Somewhere where I can feel proud every time I save a penny because it's wanted. Of course I wouldn't want my children's mother to be ill like poor Mrs. Elton, but it must be grand having so much responsibility in your first job."

Sarah laughed and pulled her arm.

"Come on, it's too cold to stand about making speeches about what you want to do. Besides, you can get that kind of job if you want to. The world must be full of poor families just screaming for people like you."

"Oh, but I can't." Beverley strode on with a worried frown. "You see it's different for me than for you. You paid your fees at the Melford Training College, but the orphanage paid mine, and so of course I must take the very first job I'm offered so that I can start paying them back."

"I don't see that," Sarah objected. "They paid your fees because they thought you were worth training."

Beverley shook her head.

"It isn't only that. They were so much more generous than they need have been. After all, the Melford Training College is about the best, and they could have sent me to a cheap one. Then they fitted me out with all my clothes." She looked down at her brown coat. "I don't say exactly dashing clothes, but neat and serviceable, which is a good thing, I suppose, for the last thing Miss Smith said when I left the Melford College was, 'Even if you have the money, dear, never be tempted into extravagance over dress; it's wasteful, out of place and would displease your employer.' "

Sarah laughed at the exact imitation of Miss Smith's tone.

" She didn't waste time saying things like that to me. She said that to you because you're pretty. After all, if you dressed me at Molyneux I'd always look just serviceable."

They turned into Cartwright Gardens. Beverley began fumbling in her bag for her key.

"Goodness, I could do with that drink. I'm perished. The shop said this coat was guaranteed all wool, but I think the sheep it came from deceived them. I think it must have had some cotton in its system."

The hostel was typical of every establishment of its kind. It was spotlessly clean. The walls were painted in a dull, olive colour which would not show the dirt. The lounge was full of practical comfortable oak furniture, guaranteed to give a canteen look to any house. Each inhabitant had a separate bedroom. These, too, were olive green with bedspread and curtains of an imitation homespun intended to look artistic. In every room was a gas fire and ring with a shilling-in-the-slot meter. Each room, beside necessities, had one armchair and a small bookcase. Sarah came from a comfortable home in the Midlands. Her family's taste was non-existent, they used cheerfully and contentedly what various generations had left them. To her, accustomed to furniture bound to her by memories, and to pictures, however repulsive, with which she had grown up, the hostel struck a note of gloom which chilled her.

"Oh, Beverley," she said, sitting down on the bed. "I do

wish you'd get a job; it's awful for you here."

Beverley was kneeling by the gas stove. She looked up in amazement.

"Awful!" She sat on her haunches, pulled off her hat and flung it beside her. "Awful! That's all you know. All my life I've wondered how it would feel to have a room of my own. A place where I could shut the door, and nobody could come in without knocking. The orphanage was grand. If you can bring up a hundred orphans as though they were members of a family, they did, but of course you can't. Even when I was at the top of the school I never slept less than four in a bedroom. I never put out my own light." Her voice dropped. "I never had a possession of my very own. Always living like that does something to you, Sarah. When I get a job, the first thing I'm going to do is to get my children independent. Independent of me and independent of everybody. Do you know, when I first went to the Melford Training College I asked a girl what time I was to go to bed. I'll never forget her face, or the way she said, 'When you like, of course. Do you expect a nanny to come and tuck you up?' I couldn't believe it when I came here; not only to go out alone, but to have a latch-key. Even now I have to give myself a dig every morning and say Get on with it, Beverley, no one is going to tell you when to get up, and no one is going to tell you whether you can have a bath or not; it's up to you.'"

Sarah looked at her fascinated. Even the cheap brown woollen frock she was wearing could not hide the fact that Beverley had a lovely figure. She had used the word pretty about her just now, but that was wrong. Beverley wasn't pretty, but she had something else. She had high cheek-bones, a pointed chin, flaming red hair, and large, grey-green eyes, too big a mouth, and a retroussé nose, but none of these things had anything to do with her quality. It was the spirit inside her which gave the effect of bubbling from a well. It was as though there was so much eagerness compressed in her small body that if she was not careful it would overflow and tip out of her hair and eyes and through her skin.

Beverley got up.

"Will you put the kettle on while I go and see if there's a letter for me? They live in a rack outside the dining-room. I always forget to look. You see, we never had any at the orphanage."

The kettle was on and the cups and saucers out when Beverley returned. She stood in the doorway. She looked so strange that Sarah was startled.

"Whatever's up?"

"I've had a letter. I've got a job."

"No! Congrats, old thing. Who with?"

Beverley sat down on the floor and held out her hands to the fire.

"Did you ever want anything awfully, Sarah, and when you got it, it was like a bad fairy overhearing your wish and giving it to you, but all wrong?"

Sarah held out her hand.

"Now, look here. I come from the Midlands, where we're plain speaking folk. If you can't tell me where the job is, let me read the letter."

5

Beverley gave herself a shake.

"Sorry." She took the letter out of its envelope. "My dear Beverley," she read, "you will be at number ten, Way Street, Piccadilly, W.I. at eleven o'clock tomorrow precisely. You will ask for Mrs. Cardew. She requires a girl of your qualifications to take complete charge of her three children, aged twelve, ten and seven. Mrs. Cardew is a professional actress, acting under the name of Miss Margot Dale, and because of this she needs someone to supervise entirely both her schoolroom and nursery. We have strongly recommended you for the position. You will kindly communicate with my secretary the moment you have seen Mrs. Cardew and tell her the result of your interview. Trusting you are well, yours sincerely, Lillian D. Smith, in brackets, principal."

"Gosh!" said Sarah. "Margot Dale! Aren't you lucky!"

Beverley hugged her knees.

"Am I? Number ten Way Street sounds rich. I wanted poor children that I could do a lot for."

"Aren't you thrilled though that it's Margot Dale?"

"No. I've heard of her, of course, but I've never seen her. I don't get thrilled about actors and actresses and people. You see, at the orphanage, we were hardly ever taken to the theatre or the pictures so we didn't get much chance to get crushes."

"But still, Margot Dale." Sarah's voice was very impressed. "After all, she's not a bit like ordinary actresses. I mean, she's a sort of genius. I've seen her in one or two plays. I saw her last in that one where she killed her husband with arsenic. I couldn't sleep for three nights. I felt just as though I had met a murderess."

Beverley got up and spooned some Horlicks into the cups and mixed the powder with cold water.

"I wonder what the children are like and whether they are boys or girls. I tell you what will be fun, and that's us meeting and comparing things. I wonder what I ought to wear. This? Or my brown silk? I'll freeze in the silk, but it is smarter."

"The kettle's boiling over," said Sarah. "I'd wear that. After all, to an actress, either of them is beneath contempt."

Beverley took the kettle off the ring and stirred the cups.

"Lucky I'm not vain." She finished mixing in silence and then held out a cup to Sarah.

Sarah took the cup and raised it.

"Here's to your job, may you get it."

Beverley lifted her cup.

"And keep it, and start paying back the orphanage." She took a sip of her milk then she raised her head, her eyes shining. "We've left out the most important bit. May the children like me."

CHAPTER TWO

THE NEXT MORNING at a quarter to eleven Beverley came out of the Green Park Station.

"Could you tell me," she asked a paper-seller politely, "which is Way Street?"

The man pointed up the road.

"See that lamp-post, you turn round there."

"Oh, do I?" said Beverley. "Then I'm early."

The paper man looked sympathetic.

"I'd wait in the Underground then. Parky for walking about. Parky for standing still if it comes to that. You thank your stars you don't have to sell newspapers on a day like this."

"Oh, I do," said Beverley. "I tell you what, I'm going to try and get a job; if I get it I'll give you sixpence when I come back, and then you can buy a cup of coffee or something. I can't give it to you now, because if I don't get the job I'll need the sixpence."

The man grinned.

"Well, that's fair. Though, mind you, though I wouldn't mind the coffee, I don't like taking the money. Anyway, here's wishing you luck."

Beverley went down to the Underground again. She tried to fix her attention on the books on the bookstall, but she couldn't. Every few minutes she was looking at her watch. Each girl who had done well at the orphanage received one of those watches as a parting gift, and as each was presented the principal said: 'And don't forget, dear,

8

tempus fugit.' "Goodness," said Beverley to herself, "I wish it would fugit a bit quicker this morning." Just before five minutes to the hour she smoothed her gloves, flicked a little bit of cotton off her coat, took a quick look in her mirror and squared her shoulders. "Now, we're off."

Way Street was one of the few bits of Mayfair that had not been converted into flats. The houses were four stories high, and all alike. The likeness did not matter, for they were built in the nicest eighteenth-century manner. The owner of the property on which the houses stood allowed no individual flourishes to mar his property, but in certain ways each family expressed its individuality. Number ten had an emerald green door, and window-boxes (although it was February) a blaze of hyacinths. Beverley, awed at the richness of the street, gave the bell a timid push. It was opened by a butler. Butlers, if you are not used to them, give a feeling of inferiority. Beverley felt very inferior. She was not only not used to butlers, but had never in her life spoken to one. To her annoyance, embarrassment took away her voice. She opened her mouth to talk and not a sound came. Angry with herself, she cleared her throat as if it were just a little hoarseness and lifted her chin proudly.

"Is Mrs. Cardew in?"

"Are you the young lady who is expected?"

"I expect it's me," said Beverley, getting over her shyness. "I know I'm expected at eleven, but it might be someone else, mightn't it?"

The butler was not prepared to bandy words with a governess, and especially with one who was not yet engaged.

"You are here about the situation as governess for the children?"

"That's right. I've been sent by the Melford Training College."

The butler said no more but led the way over a very squashy jade green hall carpet to a small sitting-room.

"You will wait here," he said, and closed the door.

The sitting-room was obviously the kind of room kept for people to wait in. It did not look as if anyone had ever sat there long or for pleasure. The chairs and table were steel, the chairs upholstered in the same jade green as the carpet. Beverley sat gingerly on the edge of one of the chairs and waited. There is nothing so depressing as waiting alone when you are nervous. Beverley waited for three quarters of an hour. She had no need to look at her own watch, a large chromium clock on the mantelpiece slowly dragged out the minutes. The room was small and the windows were shut and the central heating was on and so was a large gas fire. In a very short time she found herself feeling cold about the hands and feet but hot about the head.

At last the door opened and the butler came back.

"This way, please. Mrs. Cardew will see you now."

Beverley was taken up to a bedroom, and never had she imagined a room like it. The walls were white, the floor scarlet, with here and there a white, furry rug. The ceiling was made of copper, and was hot, for it was from there the room was heated. In the middle of the room was a bed. The occupant had evidently just left it for it was not made. It was covered in something made of white fur, and the sheets and pillow cases seemed to be of crêpe de Chine. Over the bed was a shiny scarlet canopy, held up on four white pillars. On each corner of the canopy was hung a painted, grinning or scowling mask. There were more mirrors than Beverley had ever seen before and many more than she ever wanted to see again, she decided, glancing distastefully at the many reflections of herself. Her eye fastened on the dressing-table. It was made of glass and never had she seen so many bottles. Round the walls were cupboards with glass doors. At the far side of the room from where she had come in was another door, and from behind it she heard splashings and a female voice.

"My dear Winkle, don't argue with me. I know perfectly well I never told the wretched man I'd lunch with him. I may have said I would one day, but that's no excuse for making an appointment on Friday. You must get me out of it again."

A telephone-bell began to ring. Beverley peered round the bed and saw a white receiver. She was just wondering whether prospective governesses should answer telephones, when the door of what she took to be the bathroom because of the splashings, opened, and a woman dashed in and picked up the receiver.

"Miss Dale's secretary speaking. Who is it, please? What? Oh, did she? Well, I'll go and find out; will you hold on, please?"

"Who is it, Winkle?"

The woman put her hand over the receiver and walked

to the door, trailing the lead behind her.

"It's Lady Carl's secretary; she says that at that committee the other day you said you would say a prologue at the matinée, and could you say what you're going to wear because of the curtains." There was an angry splutter from the bath.

"Aren't people inconsiderate? As if I could I know now what I'm going to wear. The prologue isn't even written. George said he would write something, but you know what George is."

Winkle stood firmly in the doorway.

"I do see that, Mrs. Cardew, but you know they have got to get on with the curtains and you won't like it if they don't go with your dress."

"Of course they've got to go with my dress. What I thought I'd do, as it's for a crèche, was to have something rather Madonna-ish and bring all the children on. I could fit the children in with whatever he writes; I mean they might be beggars or pieces of pottery or anything like that."

"How about seeing if they could get black curtains?" Winkle suggested. "That would go with anything. It would be particularly lovely if you were to appear as pottery."

"All right, tell them black." There was a sound of a tap being turned on, and over the rushing water the voice shouted, "But, Winkle, tell them if I change my mind they'll have to change the curtains."

Winkle closed the door and took her hand off the mouthpiece.

"Mrs. Cardew's secretary here. She says thank you so much for ringing up and would you please try and get black as she hadn't quite decided on the design for her dress and says she knows black would look lovely with anything." With a sigh she put down the receiver and, looking up, saw Beverley.

Winkle had grey hair drawn neatly into a minute bun. She was short and rounded, not built on the best lines for the rather masculine coat and skirt, shirt and tie that she wore. She had a face which constant need to please had creased into lines of permanent anxiety. She was short-sighted and wore horn-rimmed glasses; the glasses were intended for close work so that for an object even a short way off she pulled them forward and peered over the top of the lenses. She looked at Beverley over the top of them.

"Oh, my dear, you've come about the place as governess, haven't you? Mrs. Cardew won't be long. She's had a terribly busy morning dictating letters to me, but she won't be a minute now, I'm sure. I'll call Marcelle, her maid." She pressed the bell by the bed.

Marcelle was a gaunt woman from the Midi. She had black hair and flashing boot-button eyes. In the compression of her lips and the composure of her movements she showed the axis on which her life revolved—money. Her lady might be difficult. There were objections to this situation as there were to every situation. Her lady was temperamental and late at nights, but there were pickings. A rich widow like Mrs. Cardew was a catch in any case, but with the glamour of the stage added she was an enormous catch. Never had Marcelle known a house where so many gentlemen sent flowers and messages and would like to visit. Never was there a better position for picking up small sums of money. All the gentlemen got to know her, for often she went with her lady to the theatre. Of course at the theatre there was that horrible Mrs. Brown, the dresser, but a creature like Mrs. Brown had no understanding. It was not easy for Mrs. Brown to talk Mrs. Cardew into lunching or taking supper with someone. But she, Marcelle, could; over hairbrushings and dressings she could slip in a few words, and the gentlemen knew that, and valued her help with anything from half a crown to a pound note.

"Marcelle," said Winkle, "do you think you could get Mrs. Cardew out of her bath? This is the young lady who has come about the position as governess. Her appointment was at eleven."

Marcelle cast an eye over Beverley. It was an eye calculated to make the proudest person feel a worm; it took in her coat, hat, gloves, bag, shoes, stockings, and estimated to a farthing what the whole lot had cost, and it also stated clearly what position in the world she considered governesses held, and that was a very low position indeed, but she said nothing and went straight into the bathroom.

Beverley found herself alone once more, for Winkle bustled after Marcelle to the bathroom. Beverley was feeling more and more startled. Few people would be accustomed to a household like Mrs. Cardew's, but to Beverley, brought up in an orphanage, it did not seem real; it was as if she had stepped into a film. She felt, too, vaguely embarrassed at being in the bedroom, for surely Mrs. Cardew must be going to dress before she saw her. It must be a mistake showing her in here. Nervously she looked round the room. On either side of the mantelpiece was a low, lacquer shelf, on which were photographs of incredibly good-looking people. Women with eyelashes like lead pencils, and men, mostly photographed in profile, with exquisitely clear-cut noses and chins. Each photograph was signed across the corner, to darling, or dearest, or the one and only Margot, from so-and-so. There were also unsigned photographs of someone Beverley supposed must be Mrs. Cardew in her various acting parts. There were pictures of the same woman in crinolines and bustles, and as Lady Macbeth, as well as in modern dress. In the corner were photographs which really interested Beverley. They showed the same woman with her children. They had been taken at various dates from the time when there seemed to be only one baby, to the time when that baby seemed to have reached a long-plait stage. The photograph she guessed must he the most recent, as the ages seemed about right, showed the three children and their mother in some immense garden, the children in the exceedingly I-do-like-children-to-look-natural-in-photographs clothes, fashionable at the moment. All the three had on shirts and immaculate shorts. Beverley, peering hard at the photograph with an experienced eye, shook her head. "I bet those were put on for show; I don't believe the kids ever played in those," she thought. She turned, for the bathroom door was opening.

Margot, when Beverley first saw her, was nearing forty. She never put her age in *Who's Who,* and suggested that she had been married at seventeen and was now about thirty-one. A few catty friends observed that if this was true Margot was making a success of Portia when she was about ten. They never said it to Margot.

Genius is a misused word, but there was a grain of truth in it being applied to Margot. Her acting was uneven, she was capable of giving a wretched performance, but she was equally capable on her day of giving a performance which had in it such greatness that it lifted the woman she was playing out of her grease-paint and lights and made her almost unbearably a thing of flesh and blood. There are people who hold that greatness in an art excuses any flaw of character. Margot needed a lot of excusing. She had been a pampered only child and spoilt. Her father, a publican, had thought nothing too good for his Margot. She had been the idol of London from the time she was nineteen. From babyhood upwards Margot had been a supreme egotist. As a small child she had hysterics if she saw another child even for a moment the centre of the picture. As she grew up her ego grew with her. The stage and her really fabulous success fed her belief in herself. Even with most of London at her feet, she could not and would not endure those around her to take the faintest interest in any other person if she were present.

At twenty-five she married. She fell desperately in love with all the emotion in her overcharged body with George Cardew. George was rich and good-looking; he got his handsome income from tobacco, and his pleasure from motor-racing. Until he met Margot he had lived in a sunny dream, but having met her it was as if a door opened and let in reality. He worshipped her and thought it was the happiest day in his life when he married her. Jealousy is of all evils the most insidious. Somehow George had missed the fact that Margot was possessive and jealous. Margot carried on with her career and after the first year of marriage he got into the habit of spending his evenings with his old friends. That was the beginning of the end; scene followed scene. George, still in love, could not stand the strain; he took to drinking. Whether it was drink or a kind of desperation caused by what's-it-matter-anyway, he lost his cunning at racing, was reckless where he had been brilliant, and just six years after their wedding he crashed and was killed.

Though Margot was to blame, no one could help pitying her. The violence of her emotion kept her off the stage for nearly a year. She came back to her public with new lines of suffering on her face, and when in the mood, an ability for tragic acting even greater than she had before.

Beverley, standing in the middle of the room, stared at Margot. This was obviously the woman of the photographs, though now her head was tied up in a piece of georgette and her hair did not show. She was wearing a white satin dressing-gown. Without paying the slightest attention to the fact that anyone was in the room she climbed back into bed.

"Marcelle, bring me my drink. Winkle, telephone Peter Crewdson and tell him I shall be rather late for lunch and he'd better come round here and fetch me." She looked up and saw Beverley. She nodded graciously. "How do you do. You've come about being governess to my children, haven't you? I forget your name, but then I never have a memory for names. I can only remember it began with an A. Andrews, isn't it?"

"Shaw," Beverley muttered.

"Marcelle, Winkle, somebody, give Miss Shaw a chair."

Winkle produced a chair and put it by the bedside.

"Shall you want me, Mrs. Cardew?"

Margot shook her head.

"No. I'll see Miss Shaw alone. Oh, you two haven't met. This is Miss Winks, Miss Shaw." The door was shut and Margot and Beverley were left alone. Margot rummaged on a bedside table. "Somewhere there is a little slip of paper with the things I want to ask you; would you mind looking? I know I had it this morning because Winkle gave it to me. It's written on the back of a dressmaker's bill."

Beverley began searching the table and she saw a scrap of paper sticking out of a book.

"Is this it?"

"Oh, how clever of you, yes." Margot settled back again in her pillows. "First, how old are you?"

"Twenty-one."

Margot frowned.

"That's rather young, but my doctor wants me to have someone young for the children. He says they want to be played with. Now what comes next? Oh, yes, what religion are you?"

18

"Church of England."

"That's splendid. I don't really mind, but Winkle says that Roman Catholics made it difficult about fish and Mass. I know all about your qualifications; the College told me about them. I understand you are very clever. You are prepared to start at eighty pounds a year. Now I've got to tell you what I want. I've got three children. Meggie is twelve, Betsy ten, and David seven. They have had a nurse up till now and the two girls have been going to school, but really it has been terribly unsatisfactory. I've sent them to four different schools and each time I've had to take them away because the headmistresses have been so frightfully tiresome. They grumble because I keep them at home for a day or two, but after all they are my own children, and if I want to I don't see why I shouldn't. Then they are simply maddening about uniform. I quite see that they may like uniform, and I am quite willing to buy it, but I'm not always willing to have the children wear it. There are times when I think it's bad for their personalities to be put into the same clothes day after day, and then I say, 'No uniform for a week,' and after all, they are my children and if I feel no uniform for a week that ought to be that, but headmistresses are so difficult, so I thought I'd have a governess and then all that silly fuss is done away with."

There seemed a pause so Beverley broke in.

"Will the nurse be here if you should engage me?"

"No. You'll see her today. I'll get Winkle to take you up and introduce you to the children, but the nurse is going. What girls of twelve and ten need is a really good maid

19

who understands looking after their skin and hair, so I've got a good children's maid coming who is to be trained under Marcelle. Marcelle is a perfect devil, but worth her weight in gold. Do you think you'd like to come to me?"

Round Beverley like a pack of cards all her dreams were tumbling. Had she trained at the College in order to teach girls who needed maids to look after their hair and complexions? Had all her ideas of being helpful got to be buried in this house, where education obviously counted for nothing, where money didn't matter? Then she thought of the salary; it was higher than she had expected; with care she could repay the orphanage in under five years. She could not, in honour, turn the offer down.

"I'm sure I would like it very much. When would you like me to come?"

"Oh, at once. Let me see, today's Friday, I'd like you to come on Monday. Now I'll ring for Winkle; you'll fix everything with her."

Winkle took Beverley to her office.

"Sit down, won't you, dear. I've just got one or two things to say before we go up to the nurseries. First of all, do you want a special night out?" Her tone of voice said plainly I do hope not, but the Melford College had instilled firm principles into its pupils, one of the most important being that certain things are governesses' rights, and everybody who gave in about a right made things more difficult for others.

"Thursday, if you please, if it's convenient. I've got a friend called Sarah who's a governess and she gets Thursdays and I don't think she can change, because she's

20

working for a poor clergyman with an invalid wife, and Thursday's the only day he doesn't have choir practice or boys' clubs or something."

Winkle nodded; her voice was anxious but sympathetic.

"I do see; you mustn't think I don't. It's only that Mrs. Cardew isn't the sort of person who remembers things like half-days. If she wants something done with the children on a Thursday, and you weren't there, I'm afraid she would get upset. However, I'm sure we'll manage; we must arrange things between us. And now about the children. I've thought I ought to warn you that they are very upset at their old nurse leaving, and I'm afraid they may blame you. It's difficult for children to understand, you know."

Beverley laughed.

"I shan't worry about that. I can't expect them to like me straight away. Why should they? Has Nurse been with them all their lives?"

"Yes. She and I are the oldest inhabitants. The servants change very often. It's difficult always to please Mrs. Cardew."

"Why is she leaving now; because the children are too old?"

"Not altogether, but that's partly it of course. Really it's because Nanny was taking rather much upon herself. Sometimes she treated the children as her own, and quite defied Mrs. Cardew. Of course, that couldn't last."

Beverley nodded. Difficulties between governesses and their employers had been the subject of various lectures at the College; the tactful way in which to work the parents

21

round rather than flaunting your opinion at them.

Winkle got to her feet.

"Well, dear, I'll take you up. I do hope you'll be happy. You're very young and—" She broke off and hesitated. "I do hope you'll look on me as a friend, and come to me with any little difficulties; anything we can smooth out without referring to Mrs. Cardew—" She broke off again. "Oh, well, you'll see."

"There is a lift," said Winkle, climbing the stairs, "but we never use it, because it stops outside Mrs. Cardew's room. The children are at the top of the house. I'm afraid it's rather a climb."

In order to keep the house quiet, the nursery and the children's and nurse's bedrooms were all confined to the top floor. The servants slept on the third floor and in the basement. It was like coming into a different world, climbing the last flight of jade green staircase. First there was a gate, presumably thought Beverley, the gate must have been put up to prevent the children from falling down the stairs. Now they were past the falling stage it was shut, as if deliberately, to cut off the children's world from the rest of the house.

"They'll be in the nursery. I know Nurse said it was too cold to go out," said Winkle.

They went up the passage over bright, orange cork carpet, and Winkle opened a door.

The nursery had the same cork carpet as the passage, and walls and ceiling of the same colour. In the centre of the ceiling was painted a golden sun with rays stretching to the corners of the room. The furniture was of modern

22

fumed oak covered in bright scarlet oilcloth with yellow spots; the huge windows looking on to the front of the house were curtained, and the cushioned window-seat was upholstered in the same material as the chairs. Round the walls ran three low, scarlet bookcases, with the names of the three children written in gold on each. In the middle of all this modernity, darning by a modern fire-place surrounded by an old-fashioned nursery guard, sat a nurse who would not have been out of place in the Victorian era. A round, starched, flat-footed Nanny, of the type that has given English Nannies an unshakable niche all over the world. At the fumed oak table in the centre of the room were the three children; they were painting.

"This is Miss Shaw," said Winkle. The heads of the three children were raised from their books. "Come here, dears, and let me introduce you."

The three children grudgingly stood up and glowered at Beverley. Beverley looked at them with interest. Meggie, the eldest, had a sallow, oval face, astonishing eyes that seemed almost Mediterranean blue, and brown plaits falling to her waist. Betsy already showed she was the type who, when she grew up, would be described as an English rose. She had almost white gold curls falling just below her shoulders, a pink and white complexion and large harebell blue eyes. The boy was the beauty of the family; one of those incredibly good-looking children who make everybody say, "What a pity he isn't a girl." He had dark hair, left rather long, falling in a curling mass towards his eyebrows, huge dark brown eyes and skin the colour of a nectarine ripened on a wall. The clothes of the

23

children enhanced their looks. Meggie was in a soft, rose pink, Betsy in a shade of blue to match her eyes, and David not in the usual little masculine shirt and tie of a small boy, but a wide collared affair with a big flowing bow at the neck, which made him look like a fancy dress art student.

"How do you do," said Beverley to the children generally. She did not risk shaking hands with them, as a rebuff would put her at a disadvantage. She turned and held out her hand to Nanny. "How do you do."

Nanny laid down the darning she had in her hands and stood up.

While she shook Beverley's hand she gave her a searching glance. It was a glance without any offence in it, but it seemed to bore right into her. Suddenly she smiled.

"How do you do, Miss Shaw. You'd like to see the other rooms, wouldn't you?" She turned to the children. "Get on with your painting and don't quarrel while I'm away. This way, Miss Shaw."

The children had their bedrooms side by side. Each one had light blue walls shading into darker blue ceilings on which were painted the moon and all the stars in silver. Each one had a dark blue carpet to match the ceilings. There the likeness ended. Meggie's bed had a canopy like her mother's downstairs. Both it and the dressing-table and the chairs and curtains were upholstered in cream quilted satin. Betsy's room was a mass of pale blue organdie frills. Frills on the dressing-table, frills on the bed, and over the bed was suspended a painted wood child angel. In David's room the bed was a practical divan with no frills and it and the curtains and furniture were covered in blue and white check. At a height convenient to him was a shelf round which marched small painted soldiers in the uniforms of the various branches of the British services.

"Dear me," said Beverley, feeling completely winded by the glory of the children's rooms.

"Very silly, I've always said," Nanny remarked. "All this fal-lal, stars and that, not at all what I should choose." She opened the door of a small room at the end of the passage. "This is where I sleep and where I suppose you will."

The room was such a contrast to everything else on the nursery floor that Beverley had to smile. The walls were cream, there was a simple iron bedstead. The bedspread and curtains were of a serviceable dark repp and the furniture was a very nasty suite in modern mahogany. Nanny looked round her complacently.

"I like this room better than anywhere else in the house. Homely, that's what I call it. I never can get used to all this oilcloth everywhere, shiny cold stuff."

Beverley wondered how she could tactfully bring the subject round to the children.

"Are the children strong?"

"Well, Meggie is a bundle of nerves, takes after her mother, you know. If she's kept quiet and leads a sensible life she's all right, but there isn't any sensible life in this house. Betsy suffers from her stomach; you want to watch her food. When you know what she's having, she's all right; the trouble is to know what she's having. It's these meals out when you can't watch them. You have to watch

25

David for colds, they are apt to go to his chest. He oughtn't to go out when the weather's bad. It's hard to keep them well in the winter. If you see they are all right that's not to say their mother won't have them at one of her shows stripped almost naked."

"Do they go out with their mother a lot then?"

"That's the trouble. You see, she likes them acting in charity shows and that. Publicity, she calls it. Well, it may be good publicity, but it's bad for the children, that's what I'm always telling her."

Beverley swallowed a smile. Why Nanny was going was clear even without what Winkle had said.

"What about their clothes? Who looks after them and decides what they are going to wear?"

"All their clothes are chosen by their mother, but unless she sends up special I've always told them what to put on. There's the new maid coming who'll look after them, but you want to keep a close eye on them; if Betsy had her way she'd be getting up in velvet for the morning. Proper little miss for her clothes Betsy is."

Beverley sighed.

"I wish you weren't going. It would be much nicer for me if you were here, then I could just have taken the children for their lessons."

Nanny shook her head.

"No, it's better as it is. I've been here since Meggie was six weeks old and I couldn't stand anyone else interfering with them. Besides, it's time I had another baby; I'm taking one from the month. Little babies are my work. These children are too big for me now." She swallowed.

"Not but what I'm going to miss them." She raised eyes dimmed with tears to Beverley. "I feel better about leaving them now I've seen you; you look the understanding kind, and that's what needed in this house. You'll see."

Beverley, following Winkle downstairs, turned over Nanny's last words in her mind, "You'll see." First Winkle had said it, and now Nanny. There was something oddly sinister about the repeated phrase.

"Good-bye, my dear," said Winkle. "I shall look forward to seeing you on Monday. I hope you'll he happy here."

A sudden thrill went through Beverley at the thought that her training, the exams she had passed, and all her dreams for the future, were now to be put to the test. She raised her chin.

"I hope the children will be happy with me. That's what really matters."

As Beverley went out through the front door she passed a young man coming in. He stood back to let her go by; thinking of the work ahead of her she scarcely noticed him. He, however, came into the hall with his eyebrows raised inquiringly.

"Who's Joan of Arc, Winkle?"

Winkle laughed.

"Joan of Arc! That's the children's new governess."

He whistled.

"Is she? Well, as sure as my name is Peter Crewdson that's the young woman to lead a crusade. She ought to wear armour."

Outside the Green Park Station Beverley pause by the

27

paper man and put a sixpence in his hand.

"You got it, did you?" He put the sixpence in his pocket. "Thank you kindly. I hope it turns out a bit of all right."

Beverley's eyes looked out over the Green Park.

"Oh, so do I."

CHAPTER THREE

THE CHILDREN were out with a maid when Beverley arrived, so she took the opportunity to unpack. Unpacking for Beverley was not a long job; she had pitiably few things. There were the clothes she had had while she was training at the college; they were old and shabby now— three years of sitting and studying in them had made them shiny on the seat and baggy at the knees. She had, too, her gym tunic; it was fun to have played hockey for the college, but looking at the tunic now her face was rueful. She had taken it with her because she had nowhere to leave it, but it was not likely to be much use in Way Street. There were two new frocks of her outfit, the brown wool which she had on, and the brown silk. As well, packed amongst layers of tissue-paper, was her pride, an evening dress. Most of the girls at the college had been as poor as she was, and an evening dress had not been a necessity, but now, as she was going into a situation, the orphanage had bought her one: "You never know that you may not need it. Sometimes an employer will require the governess to make up the numbers at table; you should have the right dress to wear if this should occur." The right dress was not very grand—it was a simple, artificial silk marocaine, discreetly high at the neck, discreetly unfashionable in the sleeve-length, held demurely in place with a silver girdle. To Beverley the dress was splendid beyond dreams. She had never known people with money, and had no idea what a good dress could look like; that it was an evening dress at all was enough for her.

She had a few little things to make her room look homelike. There was the silver clock she had won for the tennis doubles at the college, there were two or three snapshots of herself and some of the other students in small frames, there were various knick-knacks she had been given for birthdays or Christmas. When she had unpacked she looked round with a sigh of content. She saw nothing lacking in her possessions; she only saw a little room which was hers and which from now onwards she could call home. She went to the window and looked down into the street. Across the way was a tree, its stark branches soot-caked. Beverley caught her breath with delight; she had known she looked out at the back on some grey houses, but she had not known about that tree. Although she could not see it, the buds must be already swelling—in no time now there would be green leaves. Her eyes shone. How lucky, how very lucky she was to get a nice bedroom like this and a tree.

She heard the children come in just as she had finished. She combed her hair and powdered her nose, then went along the passage to the nursery. She put her hand on the handle and took it back in dismay; the door was locked. Quietly she dropped her hand and stood thinking. Suppressed giggles from the other side showed her that her footsteps had been heard and so had her hand on the handle. She pictured those three on the other side—the expectant faces, the nudges, the childish cruelty that would make them gloat at her awkwardness and dis-comfiture, then with a quiet smile she walked away and tiptoed back to her room. The children could sit behind that locked door as long as they liked; she was neither going to cajole nor anything else.

Half an hour went by. Beverley, with her door ajar, pretended to read a book, but her ears were strained to listen. Suddenly she heard footsteps on the stairs—somebody was coming up. She hurried out into the passage and ran into a maid with a tray of things to lay for lunch. Beverley had never seen the maid before and felt awkward; a governess's position with the servants is very delicately balanced. Every governess knows that she must put her feet firmly in the position which is her right, and however much pushing and shaking there may be, never give an inch. Now she raised her voice so that it would carry beyond the locked nursery door.

"I'm afraid you won't be able to lay lunch. The children seem to have locked themselves in. Perhaps you will give me a tray in my room."

"Locked!" The maid's jaw dropped. "Well, I never! But what about their lunch? They can't go hungry, poor little things."

Beverley's eyes twinkled. She gave the maid a you-and-I-understand-each-other smile.

"They'll come out, I expect, when they're hungry, and if they're not hungry they can wait till tea-time." The maid caught on. She grinned and looked expectantly at the nursery door, from behind which came violent whisperings.

"Pity. There's roast chicken and they're partial to that."

The whispers grew louder and turned to mutters.

"But I am hungry."

"And it's chicken, Meggie."

"You lily-livered loons. All right, then."

There was the sound of the turning key and the door was flung open. Meggie, who had opened it, said nothing, but turned away and crouched on the window-seat, staring into the street.

"We wouldn't have come out unless we wanted to," said Betsy. "You didn't make us."

David looked at the maid.

"Is it really chicken, Mona?"

Mona bustled in and laid the cloth.

"That's right, Master David. What you want to act up so silly for, I can't see."

David sat down at the table and gazed up at her.

"Can't you?" He lowered his voice. "She's on the spot. If she's wise she'll get out while she has the chance."

"Such foolishness," said Mona, clattering knives and forks into place and not attending to him.

"Has the children's maid arrived? " Beverley asked her.

"No. Coming tea-time." Mona silently added up the forks, her lips moving as she counted.

Beverley, with a sigh, looked round at the children.

"Well, as your maid isn't here you'll have to see to yourselves. Will you all go and wash and brush your hair?"

Meggie turned her head and spoke over her shoulder:

"I don't think we will, will we?"

Beverley looked at Mona.

"Don't bring up the chicken until I ring."

Mona glanced round the nursery, amusement in every line of her. This would make good telling downstairs. Miss Shaw might be only a scrap of a thing, but she was no fool. She wouldn't like her job, but if anybody could manage these kids, she probably could. She nodded cheerfully.

"Very well, Miss Shaw."

Meggie got up. She came across to Betsy and gave her sleeve a tug.

"Come on. We don't want to sit here all day. Come on, David."

David glowered at Beverley.

"People have been bumped off for less."

"Shall I bring up the chicken?" said Mona as the door shut.

"Not till I ring. I've got to see those hands and hair first."

Mona turned to the door.

"Miss Meggie is properly riled. She's a terror when she's like that. Got a bit of her mother in her, I should say."

Mona had been helpful and Beverley did not want to snub her, but at the same time she did not believe in gossiping with the maids about any of her employer's family.

"All children are difficult sometimes," she said lightly, and went over to examine the books in Meggie's bookcase.

The three children reappeared washed and brushed, and the food was brought up. It was a most depressing lunch for Beverley. She only made one remark and, seeing how it was received, she sat the rest of the meal in silence.

"Do you say grace before meals?" she asked before they sat down.

Meggie turned to Betsy.

"Did you hear that? I thought everybody said grace unless they were heathen."

"I wouldn't wonder if she was," said Betsy. "Perhaps when she isn't here she wears nothing but beads and worships idols." They all giggled infuriatingly.

David leaned back in his chair.

"I dare say she's a cannibal. Tears children up and cooks them for dinner."

Beverley folded her hands.

"For what we are about to receive may the Lord make us truly thankful. Amen."

She tried not to mind being ostracized during the meal, but she felt oddly upset. One advantage of an orphanage is that there are always plenty of people to talk to; and there had been plenty of people at the college and even at the hostel. This sitting in silence and being talked at was very depressing. The children between them discussed her appearance, her clothes, and how much nicer Nanny had been. It was this last that gave her the first clue to any of them.

"Do you suppose," said Betsy, "she'll want to go to church on Sunday evenings like Nanny did, or is she too much of a heathen for that? And if she does go, do you think she'll wear a brown felt like Nanny's and carry a Bible full of pictures?"

Beverley, looking round the table to see if the children had nearly finished their apple-tart, caught a tightening of the muscles round Meggie's mouth. The child dropped her head almost at once and screwed her bread into pellets, but before it was dropped she had a chance to see that her eyes were full of tears. Not by a movement did she give away that she had seen; she waited a moment or two until the last spoon was put down, then got up and said grace.

After lunch she went down to Winkle. She knocked timidly on her office-door, and was reassured by a hearty "come in".

"I'm sorry to bother you, Miss Winks."

Winkle looked up from the papers she was sorting. "It's no bother; sit down."

"I can't wait, thank you. I've got to go back to the children. What do they do in the afternoons? Winkle pulled her glasses forward and looked over their rims.

"That's difficult to say. You see, they should be at school. Aren't you going to teach them?" Beverley leaned against the desk.

"I can't today; they aren't speaking to me." Winkle made clicking disapproval sounds with her tongue.

"Dear, dear, dear. How very tiresome of them. Would you like me to come up to see if I can do anything with them?"

"No. It would be fatal. I just want to know what's the right thing to do. Should I take them for another walk?"

Winkle glanced out of the window.

"I hardly think so. It's very grey and it gets dark so early at this time of the year."

"All right, as long as I know whether they ought to be out or in. If it's in I can handle them."

Winkle blinked.

"I do hope so, dear, and don't forget, whatever you do, come to me and not to Mrs. Cardew; though mind you it might be a good thing to threaten you'll go to her."

Beverley shook her head.

"Not me," she grinned. "'Never threaten what you don't intend to carry out.' That's one of the things we learnt at Child Guidance. Don't worry. I'll manage."

Upstairs the nursery looked a picture of what a nursery ought to look. Meggie was sitting on the window-seat reading; Betsy and David were playing snap. They none of them looked up as she came in.

Beverley had brought a piece of sewing with her. She sat quietly down in Nanny's chair by the fire. She got up with a yelp. Upright on the seat someone had stuck a pin. The children howled and rocked with laughter. Furious with herself for having yelped, and longing to knock the children's heads together, Beverley savagely extracted the pin and sat down again.

The afternoon ticked wearily away; there was a certain amount of pointed conversation amongst the children, but not a word was addressed to Beverley. Tea, though it was taken in stony silence on Beverley's part, came as a relief.

"The new maid's here," said Mona, when she came to clear away. "She says will you see her now?" Beverley got up.

"I'll see her in my room."

It felt positively exhilarating talking to the new maid.

She had never been silent for so long before and her tongue ached with repression. The maid's name was Annie; she was round, shiny-cheeked, and very friendly.

"You just tell me exactly what's wanted, Miss, and I'll manage. I've been children's maid for a year, only the young ladies were growing up and wanted a real maid. I'm to learn here under Mrs. Cardew's maid, Marcelle. Do you know what she's like, Miss?"

Beverley shook her head.

"I'm new here. I've seen her, she's French."

"Did she look easy?" said Annie. "Her ladyship in my last place she had a proper termagant of a maid; no matter what you did you were always wrong."

Beverley had a strong feeling that whatever Annie did would be wrong under Marcelle too, but she kept her ideas to herself.

"I expect it will be all right here. I don't suppose you'll see much of Marcelle; she's always busy with Mrs. Cardew."

"Don't know so much," said Annie gloomily. "I'm to do my sewing under her. What do the young ladies wear in the evening, Miss?"

Beverley knew by now that all the servants would have heard of the children's naughtiness and would doubtless tell Annie directly she got down to the servants' hall. She laughed.

"I've no idea. They're being naughty today. They didn't want their nurse to leave, and they didn't want me to come, so they won't speak. You can go in and try though."

"Not me." Annie shook her head. "Eldest of seven I am,

and if there's one thing you do learn in a big family it's not to give in to any playing up. All that lying down and screaming and such gives me the sick."

Beverley felt her heart warming. The house might be grand and unfamiliar, and the children difficult, but here at last was an ally.

"Well, go and turn their beds down," she suggested. "I dare say if they're going to change they'll come and tell you."

She hurried up the passage with a lighter heart. Quite gaily she opened the nursery door. Inside, she stood still in dismay. While she had been gone the children had smeared the outer door handle with ink. There was ink all over her right hand, but that didn't matter; somehow in passing the handle had rubbed on her dress.

Red hair had not been given to Beverley for nothing. Her first inclination was to cry, which would have been fatal; fortunately for her, temper dissolved the lump in her throat.

"You little horrors!" she blazed. "You smug, detestable little beasts! Just because you've been brought up having every single thing you want, does that mean you've no imagination at all? I've seen your cupboards and I know just how many clothes you little toads have got, but I'm poor and was brought up in an orphanage, and I've only got two good dresses, and this is one of them and you've spoilt it—"

The three children stared at her, their eyes rounded with amazement. Suddenly their expressions changed.

"Peter!" said Meggie.

Beverley, her face crimson, turned. In the doorway was the young man she had passed when she came for her interview. She had been too engrossed to notice him then; now, sunk in depths of mortification, she looked at him, and found herself gazing into a pair of twinkling grey eyes.

"This is our new governess," said Meggie. "She's a nice sort of governess. She called us little horrors."

"And toads," David chimed in.

Betsy stood on one leg and held the other.

"And she said we were smug and detestable little beasts."

Peter shut the door, came in, and sat on the table. He was tall, well over six feet, sandy haired, with unusually well-cut features. He looked round at the young Cardews, collecting them with his eyes.

"It is delightful," he remarked at last, "to hear the dear little Cardews told what they are like. I've been wanting to do it for years."

"Peter, you haven't!"

"You like us awfully."

"He's only pretending."

Peter's face was grave.

"As a matter of fact I do like you when you behave yourselves, but I never knew a trio that could be such cads as you can when you try. What have you been up to?"

There was an awkward silence, broken at last by Betsy.

"We didn't want to have a governess."

Meggie crossed the room and stood beside Peter. "We didn't mean the ink to go on her frock, only on her

39

hands."

Peter turned and glanced at Beverley's skirt.

"You seem to have mucked it up pretty well." He caught hold of both Meggie's plaits and pulled her round to face him. "Come on, young woman, confess." Meggie wriggled, but he held on. "No, I'm not letting go. What have you been up to?"

"We hoped she'd go," she growled in a surly voice. "It isn't her, it's anybody. What do we want a governess for? We were all right as we were."

He gently let the plaits drop.

"All right! Never learning anything. Besides, you're not showing much perspicacity. It's a long word and it means ability to think things out. First and foremost, if ever a girl needed taking in hand you do, and you ought to know it; secondly, one look at your governess ought to have shown you that she is not the kind of woman to be scared off by a few kids playing practical jokes." He got up. "Well, that's the end of tonight's bedtime talk. Good night, children."

Betsy flung herself at him.

"You're not going, Peter. You'll stay and play rummy with us."

He picked her off him as if she were a limpet and he a rock.

"Not me. I'll come another day, and if I get a good account of you from Miss—" He glanced at Beverley with raised eyebrows.

"Shaw."

"From Miss Shaw I'll stay, but I've got a very big calling list and I don't include ink-throwers amongst my friends."

40

As the door shut there was an awkward silence.

Meggie scratched at the carpet with her toe.

"If you changed I expect Marcelle has got something that would take that out." She scowled, framing her words awkwardly. "As a matter of fact we're sorry. I mean we didn't mean it to get on you, and anyway, we didn't know you were poor and all that."

Beverley nodded.

"That's all right. As a matter of fact, Annie, your new maid, has arrived; I'll see if she can do something. Meanwhile, you can get some blotting-paper and clean the door handle."

Annie helped Beverley out of her frock and into her artificial silk.

"I've got some stuff that's good for ink, and this is only a surface smear; it might come out. Anyway, you leave it to me, Miss, and I'll try."

Back in the nursery, the children were in a knot in front of the fireplace, whispering. They looked up as Beverley came back.

"Can she get it out?" asked Meggie.

Beverley shrugged her shoulders.

"She isn't sure, you know how it is with ink. Luckily, it's dark and won't show much. Annie wants to know about changing. Do you change in the evening?"

"Oh, yes, always," said Betsy. "I'm going to wear my pink taffeta tonight."

Meggie looked contemptuous.

"We've got black velvet we put on at six when we go down to Mummy. We don't wear our taffetas and things

41

like that unless we are going somewhere. David wears a silk blouse."

"You are a sneak," Betsy grumbled. "You know Mummy wouldn't have minded if I'd worn my pink."

"She wouldn't have minded to you," Meggie argued, "but she would have cursed Miss Shaw."

"Well, who cares," Betsy gave her head a toss and shook out her curls.

Beverley decided the argument had gone on long enough.

"Well, it's a quarter to six now. You and David go and change. I want a word, Meggie."

Beverley was surprised to find herself obeyed. Meggie looked stubborn, but she remained where she was while the door shut on the other two. Beverley sat casually down at the nursery table.

"Where do you do your lessons?" She looked round at the toy cupboard built at an easy height for David, at the rocking-horse, and the modern doll's house. "This is all right for David, but you're a bit big for a nursery. Haven't you got a schoolroom?"

Meggie nodded.

"It's downstairs, by the drawing-room. We've never used it except to practise our dancing; you see we've always been to school."

"I see. Well, if you show me where it is when you go down to your mother, I'll have a look round. We must start work in the morning."

Meggie scratched at the table with one of her nails.

"I expect you'll think we're stupid."

42

"I don't expect much from Betsy, and almost nothing from David, but we must try and get you on. What's your favourite subject?"

"Literature. I know most of Shakespeare's women's parts."

Beverley raised her eyebrows.

"That's more than I do. Well, run along or you'll be late."

Left alone, Beverley went round tidying the room. She felt annoyed. A grievance nagged at her. She knew it was unreasonable, but she did wish that young man Peter had not come in just then. First of all, he must think very poorly of a graduate from a teaching college who could call her pupils toads and things like that, but the worst part of it was that it was he who had tamed the children. Left to herself she was certain she would have got them to heel by the morning, but even if it had taken weeks she would rather have endured it than have had a strange young man springing to her aid. This trial of strength against the children was the first chance she had been given of proving what her training in child psychology was worth. Suddenly, she slammed the nursery cupboard, and smiled. "No good muttering round the room because he interfered, you idiot," she told herself fiercely. "You failed and you know it. What do you suppose they would say at Melford if they could have heard you calling your pupils smug, detestable little beasts?"

Beverley was not to have a chance to see the school-room that night. Just as the children were going down, the house telephone rang. It was Winkle to say that Mrs.

Cardew wished her to come to the drawing-room.

The drawing-room was a study in blue. The walls, ceiling and carpet were a pale madonna shade. The furniture was upholstered in silver. In one corner of the room was an immense silver Buddha lit by concealed lighting. Margot was lying on the sofa, wearing a trailing black frock.

"Well, how are my babies tonight? Meggie, darling, those plaits must be a little tighter; it gives such a delicious line to your head. How's my Betsy?" She held out her hand to David. "And how's my baby boy?" The children gathered round the sofa and kissed their mother. Margot smiled at Beverley. "How are you?" She turned back to the children. "Now tell me all the lovely 'citing things you've done today."

"We went in the park with Marcelle this morning," said Betsy, "and I pretended I was a fairy, and everybody I looked at was lucky."

Meggie gave an angry shrug of her shoulders.

"If you call making eyes at everybody bringing them luck."

Betsy tossed her curls.

"Fairies can do anything. It isn't making eyes if you're a fairy, is it, Mummy?"

David was jumping up and down to attract his mother's attention.

"At Hyde Park Corner there was a crowd. Marcelle said I mustn't look, but I did. I hoped it was an accident, but it was only a faint."

"And any lessons?" Margot asked.

The children gave furtive looks at Beverley. Was she going to tell? Beverley stepped forward.

"Not till tomorrow. I'm going to have a little examination in the morning to see what they all know."

Margot made a face at the children.

"Oh, dear, that sounds tellibly serious, doesn't it?" She put her arm round Betsy and drew her to the sofa. "Naughty Miss Shaw mustn't make us too clever-ums, must she?"

Meggie gave another jerk of her shoulders.

"Well, I'm twelve; I suppose I ought to know something."

Margot frowned.

"Is it that naughty black dog on your shoulder again? I don't think that's a very kind way to speak to poor Mummy."

"Goodness," thought Beverley, feeling vaguely sick, "and I was made a junior prefect when I was twelve."

"As a matter of fact," Margot went on, "there won't be a great many lessons tomorrow. We're all going to be photographed."

Betsy looked pleased, but David and Meggie groaned.

"Not again," said Meggie. "We were photographed the week before last."

David hung over the back of the sofa.

"I was sick last time."

"That, my boy, was not photographs, it was sweets," said Betsy. "You ate dozens and dozens in the car."

Margot spoke firmly.

"We're going to be nice kind people tomorrow. There's

45

a charity matinée in April in aid of poor little babies in crèches, and they want Mummy to speak the prologue and you are all going to be on the stage with me. Won't that be fun?" It was obvious from the looks on Meggie's and David's faces that they thought it would be anything but fun, but Margot swept on unmoved. "I don't know yet quite what we're going to wear, but it will be something very pretty."

"If we're being photographed tomorrow," said Meggie, "need I wear socks—I'd much rather wear stockings. I'm too big for socks, and I'm not the type."

Margot stiffened. There was an angry flash in her eyes.

"You'll wear what I say. You don't look twelve and, as a matter of fact, everybody thinks you're ten, and ten is the age I want you to look."

"Little Betsy Cardew is eight," said Betsy.

Meggie scowled.

"That's a lie. You're ten; why do you want to look eight?"

"I want to look whatever Mummy wants me to look."

She was rewarded with a smile from her mother. "Now tomorrow you're going to wear those new little frilly frocks. I've told Marcelle and she'll see that the new maid packs them. And I don't want those fastened-up socks, Betsy; little tumbled socks, and shoes with ankle-straps. David will wear the Kate Greenaway suit that he wore at the wedding."

"Then I'll certainly be sick," said David. "It's too tight and hurts my stomach."

Margot got up.

"You are the most disagreeable children. Here is poor Mummy working day and night in the theatre to buy you pretty things, and all you do is to grumble. But I'm not going to be upset, it puts me off my work when I'm upset. Take them upstairs, Miss Shaw. I don't want to see any of them again tonight. They are to be ready to go to the photographer's at eleven."

Betsy put her arms round her mother's neck.

"You aren't angry with me, Mummy?"

"Yes, I am," said Margot. "I'm angry with all of you. Now run away."

The children went to bed half an hour after each other. Annie collected them one by one. Meggie had her supper in the schoolroom with Beverley. The child had been very silent since they had come up from the drawing-room. Beverley, helping her to fish pie, wondered if she dared say anything to lead her on to discuss what she herself wanted in the way of education.

"You will have to have the examination tomorrow afternoon," she said, passing over the plate. "It's no good starting if you've all got to go out in the morning."

Meggie ate a mouthful of fish before she answered. "It's always like that. Mummy thinks lessons aren't much use."

"What do you think?" Beverley asked casually.

Meggie took a breath as if to speak; for one moment the eyes she turned towards Beverley were brimming with the words she wanted to say, then as suddenly they went dead.

"Oh, I don't know. I don't suppose they do matter much."

47

Beverley said nothing, but turned the conversation to the discussion of Shakespeare. After Meggie had gone to bed, she fetched a book she was reading from her room, and tried to concentrate on it, but it was no good. The Cardew children came between her and the pages. What on earth was she in for? A mother who treated her children as though they were pet dogs. Somehow all the training she had received had never suggested a situation like this. Methods of teaching and how to get the best out of your pupils had been the vital thing; nobody had suggested or apparently known that there might be a house where a governess was engaged only to keep the children happy.

"All the same," she thought, "it's interesting. If only I could get them to like me. I'm sure I could be some use."

If Peter Crewdson had seen her then he would certainly have called her "Joan of Arc".

CHAPTER FOUR

SARAH and Beverley met in a teashop and ordered banana splits.

"Well?" Sarah leaned forward, her chin on her hands, her eyes shining with interest. "Tell me everything. What are the children like?"

"I'm not sure. It's the most extraordinary house, Sarah. You know we always imagined fathers and mothers who were interested in the children's education, didn't we? You can't think what it's like at number ten Way Street. I've made out a time-table, of course, but it is impossible to stick to it."

"Why?"

Beverley sighed.

"If you only knew all the whys. On Tuesday it was photographs, yesterday there were people to lunch and we had to stop lessons early in order to get in from our walk in time to have the children dolled up to meet the guests. Then today, right in the middle of the morning, Mrs. Cardew brought six people in and made the children recite."

"What sort of hours are you teaching them?"

"It's rather difficult; breakfast is supposed to be nine, which is much too late. It really means you can't start lessons much before ten and I have to take them for a walk at twelve; so from ten to twelve I take all three children; then in the afternoon I send David and Betsy out with the maid, Annie, and take Meggie by herself until tea at half-past four. Really Betsy ought to be doing more lessons, but I wouldn't be able to teach Meggie a thing if I didn't have her alone."

"Are they nice children?"

Beverley smiled, and told her about her start at the house.

"What little toads," said Sarah. "How awful for you, that man hearing. Do you think he told Mrs. Cardew?"

"No, I'm sure he didn't." Beverley paused while her sundae was put in front of her. "Of course there is supposed to be a nice side to every child if you can find it, but up to date I'm having a sticky time finding the nice side of my children. Meggie is more difficult than anything you ever knew; she was fond of the nurse that left. I think she used to talk to her; she was the one person she did talk to. She reminds me of a rose that's managed to hang on to a tree all through the winter. You know, all shrivelled up and all its petals sticking together. It's impossible to get anything out of her. She's dreadfully backward, except that she knows masses of poetry and practically everything Shakespeare wrote."

"Well, that's a good start."

"Yes, but she can hardly do simple addition. She doesn't know a word of French and her handwriting would disgrace a child of six." She swallowed a mouthful of sundae. "All the same, I've a feeling I would rather like Meggie if she'd let me."

"And Betsy?"

Beverley laid down her spoon.

"I dare say you'll be shocked, Sarah, but I think she's a loathsome child. She's vain, always showing off, and doesn't care about anything at all, except her hair and her clothes, and her mother makes her worse."

"What's the boy like?"

"Well, he's only seven. I've made more progress with him than the others. You see, he's so little that it is easy to get him interested, then he forgets that he isn't liking me. I'm teaching him to read. He knows a bit, but he's slow. The only way to teach him is to get a story that interests him. I gave him, to begin with, *The Tailor of Gloucester*, but in the middle of the story he suddenly closed the book and said, Miss Shaw, if the tailor isn't going to die and that cat is going to repent, I've lost interest.'"

Sarah laughed.

"He sounds a card. What did you give him?"

"I found a simple history book with fairly vivid accounts of battles. He likes anything with some dead about."

Sarah eyed her friend.

"You look pale. Are you hating it there?"

Beverley nodded.

"I'm a weak-spirited, gutless creature, but oh, dear, I'd love to give in my notice. You can't think what it's like, Sarah. Everything in the house revolves round Mrs. Cardew. Nothing else seems to matter. And somehow it's all so soulless, everything frightfully grand, masses of servants and nobody caring twopence about real things. I believe that Mrs. Cardew would rather any of them won a beauty competition than showed signs of growing up into nice people."

Sarah set her shoulders and looked severe.

"What's the matter with you, Beverley Shaw? This seems to me the exact job for you. You said to me on the very night when you got the letter telling you to go and see Mrs. Cardew, 'I hope I get a job somewhere where I'm really needed.' My goodness, where could you be more needed? If nobody else is going to bring the children up, what a chance for you."

Beverley ate silently for a few minutes.

"It's lack of interest that's so discouraging. You see, in your vicarage, there's Mrs. Elton in her bed, just waiting for you to come in and tell her how the children are getting on, and to discuss things with you, and there's Mr. Elton never too busy to help you and talk things over; but I'm all alone, nobody cares what I teach the children, or how they grow up, as long as they're not in the way and always looking pretty."

"Aren't there any friends or relations that take an interest?"

"Mrs. Cardew doesn't see her relations. Her father's dead; he was a publican and after he died she cut off from her family."

"Weren't good enough for her, I suppose."

Beverley nodded.

"That's what's said. There's a Cardew grandmother and some Cardew aunts; I haven't seen them yet. I get all my news from Annie who gets it from the servants' hall. I don't mean that I gossip, but she chatters, you know. Annie says the servants say the children are twice as nice after they've stayed with the Cardews."

"Well, what about friends?"

"Men. I never knew anybody knew so many men. Wherever you go you pass them in the hall or on the stairs. There're just a few women, but they're ghastly— actresses and people like that."

"This Mr. Crewdson sounds all right."

Beverley nodded.

"I was rather mean in my mind about him, but I see now it was just meanness. You see, after the children had been so awful I did want it to be me who made them behave, and I grudged it being him. He was awfully nice really. We haven't seen him since. He's always in the house, but he hasn't been up to the nursery."

"What's he always doing in the house?"

Beverley flushed.

"It does sound as though I was always listening to gossip, but I can't help it, Annie just runs on. He's what she calls Mrs. Cardew's No.1 man. She says she's going to marry him."

"I thought you said he was young."

"Well, so he is, sort of twenty-six, twenty-seven, but I don't think she's more than about thirty. She married at seventeen, she told me."

"She started young then," said Sarah. "Father saw her play Perdita twenty-one years ago. She was on tour; she came to our town."

"Twenty-one years!" Beverley looked startled. "Even suppose she was seventeen, then she must be thirty-eight now."

53

"Well, I suppose ten or twelve years isn't much if you're in love. What's he like?"

Beverley put her head on one side while she considered.

"He's tall, with nondescript coloured hair and grey eyes. He's got awfully expressive hands and rather brownish skin as though he played a lot of games."

"Sounds all right. Have another sundae?"

Beverley shook her head.

"No. What I'd really like to do is to go for a walk. Could you bear to go up to Regent's Park and walk across to Primrose Hill?"

Sarah sighed.

"Gosh! It's plain you've gone into a house full of motorcars. If you were me and had to walk miles on your flat feet dragging children after you, you'd never want to walk on your Thursdays. I haven't any maid to take the younger children out."

Beverley was repentant.

"Sorry, we'll go to the pictures. It's only I felt so cooped up, shut in, and centrally heated, and I thought the wind in my face and a brisk talk with you was just what I needed."

Sarah got up and took her arm.

"Come on, you old fool. Of course we're going for that walk. If you think I'm going to let you, who've never been downed by anybody, get downed by the Cardew family in your first week, you're very much mistaken. Come on, Primrose Hill and back."

Either Primrose Hill or Sarah or both were the stimulant that Beverley needed. She came back to number ten Way Street that night in a much more courageous frame of mind, and woke up in the same state the next morning.

"I'm not going to be gutless any more," she told herself firmly in her bath. "There are one or two things in this house that have got to be put right, and I'm going to see to them." Still in the same brisk frame of mind she joined the children at breakfast. Betsy was lolling in a heap in her chair, her face greenish, with dark shadows under her eyes.

"What's the matter, Betsy?"

Betsy's head rolled over.

"I feel peculiar."

Meggie and David eyed her with experienced eyes.

"You'd better make her lie down," said Meggie. "She never gives any warning, she just is."

"On the floor, anywhere," David agreed.

Beverley put her hands under Betsy's armpits and raised her up.

"Come on, old lady, come to bed."

"If I move I'll be sick," Betsy whispered.

"No you won't. You'll lie flat on your back with a hot-water bottle and you'll feel better."

Betsy made ominous sounds.

"Open the door, Meggie," said Beverley, "and call Annie."

Just in time they got the child to her room, and after the attack was over, lying on her bed. Beverley left her to

55

Annie's administrations and went back into the nursery.

"Is she often like that?"

Maggie helped herself to some honey.

"Always if she eats too much. There was a cocktail party last night and we went down to it to hand round."

David gulped his milk.

"I thought she'd be sick in the night. I was as surprised as anything when I saw her this morning. She ate two whole plates of caviar on bread and butter and then she ate a plate of prawns and then somebody gave her a box of chocolates and she ate most of those."

"Somebody is supposed to see she doesn't," Meggie explained. "But you see you were out and Winkle was busy and she doesn't listen to anything I say."

"I never heard such nonsense. Whatever does a child of ten need watching for. If Betsy knows things make her sick she shouldn't eat them."

"But she does know," Meggie pointed out. "And she eats everything just the same."

Beverley poured herself out some more coffee.

"Well, that's her funeral. I should find it a bore being sick myself, but if she enjoys it—"

Meggie stared at her round-eyed.

"How queer you are. Nobody's ever said anything like that to us before. Children aren't supposed to look after themselves."

"That's all you know," Beverley retorted, sipping her coffee. "That's why I'm so sorry for children like you."

Meggie and David looked shocked.

"Sorry for us!"

"People never stop saying to us how lovely it must be to be Mummy's children."

"I don't care how much they say it, there's too much done for you and too much you don't do for yourselves. Mind you, I don't say it's fun being brought up like I was. You see, my mother died when I was born, and my father died very soon afterwards and there wasn't much money. My father was a doctor and an orphanage for professional people's children took me in. I was three when I went there, and, believe me, by the time I was three and a half, I was learning to take care of myself."

Meggie and David looked interested.

"You couldn't do much at three and a half," Meggie protested.

"Not much, but I was learning. I used to have awful colds and I remember going to the matron when I was about six with a particularly good streamer and matron said to me: 'You are having far too many colds, Beverley. An intelligent child would come to me at the first feeling of a cold, and it could possibly be checked. But you don't come near me until it's really bad. In future, if I have to keep you in bed for a cold, you'll only get the extra comforts of the sanatorium if you've been to me at the beginning and warned me that a cold was on its way. If you come to me in this state again, your time in bed will be treated as a punishment.' "

"How frightfully mean," said Meggie, "and you were only six."

"Mean nothing," said Beverley, reaching for a piece of toast. "It practically cured me of having colds."

David looked thoughtful.

"I rather like having colds. I've got a frightfully delicate chest which might get to pneumonia. Every time I get a cold I write a will."

Beverley laughed.

"Why a new will every time?"

"People change," he said darkly. "Sometimes they're in and sometimes they're out; you know how it is with wills."

Meggie leaned back in her chair.

"But, Miss Shaw, children have people like you to look after them; I don't see any point in the children looking out as well as the grown-ups."

Beverley laughed. "Depends what you want to grow up like. I like to see people grow up independent. I don't know any more sickening sight than women who can't take their own rug off their own knees in their own motor-cars, who can't take off their own clothes, and can't open their own front doors."

David looked up.

"Like Mummy, you mean?"

Too late Beverley saw the impression she had given.

"Of course not. Your mother is a great actress. That's different."

"What will you do for Betsy?" asked Meggie. "Just leave her to be sick?"

Beverley shook her head.

"Not this time. I'm going to her now. I shall give her a nice large dose of castor oil; there's nothing like it."

While Meggie was working out a sum, and David busy

on a copy, Beverley rang Winkle on the house phone and asked if she could see her for a minute.

"Yes, dear," Winkle chirped, "if you come straight away. I'm expecting to be rung for any minute; it's her dictating time."

Winkle was at her desk, her spectacles forward on her nose, looking harassed.

"I'm having a terrible morning. Marcelle brought a message half an hour ago that Mrs. Cardew is changing all today's plans, and I was to cancel her engagements. People are really very queer—they always seem to blame me. Such unpleasantness on the telephone! Well, what's your trouble?"

"Mine isn't exactly a trouble. Could you arrange to have the schoolroom breakfast earlier? The children don't have it until nine; it ought to be eight-thirty at the latest, if I'm to get a proper morning's work."

Winkle pulled her glasses almost to the tip of her nose.

"Oh, dear, ought it? That's the kind of thing the servants hate."

"But, Miss Winks, the servants are paid to work; surely half an hour won't hurt them."

"Of course not, dear, but you're not used to this house. The cook probably doesn't get up till quite late, and she'll complain to Marcelle, and Marcelle will tell Mrs. Cardew."

"Well, even if she does, Mrs. Cardew won't mind, will she, if it's good for the children?"

Winkle shook her head.

"It's clear you haven't understood what happens." She

lowered her voice. "Marcelle is a wonderful maid, but I cannot make myself like her. She is, I'm afraid, rather sly. What would happen would be that it will suit Marcelle to please the cook, and she'll tell Mrs. Cardew that breakfast is half an hour earlier from the children's angle; she'll say everybody says they look tired or something like that."

Beverley raised her head.

"Very well then, I shall ask Mrs. Cardew myself." She saw the scared-rabbit look in Winkle's eyes. "Don't be fussed, I'll be tactful."

When lessons were over Beverley looked in on Betsy before going out. The poor child seemed wretched. Her face was damp and green and her hair stuck in streaks to her forehead.

"I've been sick four more times," she said weakly.

Beverley, under pretence of stroking her hair, felt her forehead to see if she had a temperature. She seemed a little hot, so she decided to send for the doctor.

"You'll be better soon, old lady."

"I don't see why. The castor oil hasn't stopped inside me."

"Poor old thing. Is there anything I can do before we go out?"

"Yes. Ask Mummy to come up and see me."

"Very well, I'll ring down."

"Promise?"

"Of course. I was going to, anyway."

In the passage she switched through to Margot's room. Meggie, coming out of her room dressed to go out, looked to see what she was doing and in a bound took the receiver from her and put it back on its stand. Her face was angry.

"What are you doing?"

"My dear Meggie, it's more a case of 'what are *you* doing.' I was just getting through to your mother to tell her Betsy wasn't well and would like to see her, and might I ring up the doctor." She put her hand towards the receiver. "Any objections?"

"Yes." Meggie twisted her hands nervously. "You can't ring Mummy up about things like that. She hates people being ill. She won't come up. Betsy knows that."

"Won't come up!" There was, in spite of herself, shocked surprise in Beverley's voice.

Meggie flushed.

"She can't help it. She's different to other people. It's not that she doesn't love us. It's because anybody ill or unhappy makes her ill."

Beverley was hurt by the shamed distress in the child's face.

"I understand," she said gently. "There are people like that, I know." She was rewarded by seeing Meggie relax. "But what about the doctor? She's got a slight temperature, I think, and she can't keep the castor oil down."

"You tell Winkle. She gets the doctor."

"All right." Beverley switched the phone through to Winkle's office. "You go and tell Betsy I couldn't keep my promise and explain why."

"She knows why," said Meggie bitterly. "She only asked you to do it because she's a little beast."

The doctor was with Betsy when they came back from their walk. He met Beverley in the passage.

"Are you Miss Shaw?" She nodded. "Will you come into the nursery? I'd like a word with you."

"I'm not calling this the nursery any more," said Beverley. "They're too big—at least Meggie is; I'm calling it 'the children's sitting-room.'"

The doctor smiled.

"It's clear you're a new broom. Let me introduce myself. My name is Grey. We shall be seeing a lot of each other, I expect."

She liked the look of him. He was not young, but he had young eyes, and a cheerful friendly face—just the sort, she thought, to be a children's doctor.

"How d'you do. How is Betsy?"

He put his bag down on the table.

"If that child can't be trusted with caviare and prawns, she must not go down when there's a cocktail party. One day she'll be seriously ill."

"Yesterday was my afternoon off. I didn't know there was going to be a cocktail party. If I had I might have sent Annie, their maid, down with the children, but you know I think it's an idiotic way to bring kids up. She's ten, that child; she can't go through life with someone always by her."

He gave her an interested glance.

"They haven't had a chance, you know, poor little devils. Nurse was splendid, but all nurses try and keep their children babies, it's only natural. Their mother—" He broke off. "Even after two or three days in the house you must know that she is not always very wise with them."

Beverley grinned.

"I'd put it worse than that."

He shook his head.

"She's my patient too, and I'm not saying anything about her. Only if you're really interested in the children you might make all the difference in their lives. That child Meggie is a bundle of nerves. I've been at her mother for years to keep her quieter. See what you can do. The whole lot, especially David, want exercises; you know, real health and beauty stuff. I've told Mrs. Cardew, but nothing gets done. David wouldn't have half the colds he does if we could widen his chest a bit."

Beverley's face lit up.

"I can exercise them. It was part of my training. There's a gramophone over there. I'll have them deep-breathing and touching their toes before breakfast."

"Good." He picked up his bag. "If you don't mind a word of advice, 'walk carefully'. See if you can get the exercise idea to come from their mother." He went to the door. "I've given that maid a prescription for Betsy. I'll be in to see her in the morning."

That evening Beverley went down to Margot with Meggie and David. Ostensibly her object was to tell her about Betsy. They found Peter in the drawing-room.

"Where's Betsy?" asked Margot.

"Need you ask?" said Meggie. "Did you see what she ate at the cocktail party?"

A look of distaste slid across Margot's face.

63

"Oh, dear. How nasty."

" Sick, and sick, and sick she's been; she's brought up—" David broke off with a yelp. "Don't kick me, Meggie. I thought Mummy'd be interested. After all, it was food once."

"You know she wouldn't be, you dirty little beast," Meggie growled.

Margot held up a hand.

"David, one more horrid expression from you and you'll go back to the nursery; you've made poor Mummy feel ill." She turned to Beverley. "Did you want to see me, Miss Shaw?"

Beverley shook her head.

"Just to tell you about Betsy. She's all right now; the doctor sent round some medicine which pulled her together."

"My poor baby," said Margot. "You should be more careful, Miss Shaw. There are lots of things at parties that don't suit little insides."

"I'm sorry, but Thursday's my half-day. I wasn't there."

Margot wriggled.

"Surely it can't matter to you which day you go out. If I want you I expect you to be in, that's what I pay you for."

Peter, who was by the window, turned round.

"I expect Miss Shaw's a weak vessel like me. We haven't all got your gearing." He looked at Beverley. "Mrs. Cardew has got a non-stop engine, she never runs down, or needs days off like us lower grade cars."

Beverley could have bitten him—there he went again interfering. Could he never let her fight her own battles?

A little quiet support over the children's exercises perhaps, but this everlasting butting in was another matter.

"I also wanted to talk to you about some exercises for the children," she said, forgetting tact in her annoyance. "Meggie slouches and David is narrow-chested. I thought I'd have them up half an hour early and drill them before breakfast."

Margot flushed.

"If I want exercises I'll ask for them, and there's nothing the matter with the children. Ridiculous. Certainly they can't get up earlier; little children need a lot of sleep."

Behind Margot's back Peter wagged a finger at Beverley. He lounged over to Margot's sofa.

"They do need exercises, sweet. I heard somebody—I shan't tell you who—say the other day how queer it was that somebody with your exquisite figure didn't take more trouble with your girls'."

There was a shriek from Margot.

"Peter, you didn't. You're making it up because you know it'll hurt me. Who said it? Whoever it was, was a cat and was jealous. Meggie, stand up against the door. Let me look at your back."

Meggie was deep in *Punch* and got up scowling.

"Of course I don't stoop."

Margot looked at her with her head on one side.

"Yes, you do. You do worse, you poke. Let me look at you, David. Come here, let Mummy see if she can make your shoulder-blades meet. Now don't make that noise. I'm not hurting you; Mummy's doing it for your own good. You want to grow up a great big man like Uncle Peter, don't you, whom all the women love and who can be tellibly unkind, too. Yes, you are narrow-chested. I won't give people an excuse to say horrid unkind things about Mummy's babies. Miss Shaw, I was right, I must insist on exercises, and whether you like it or not you must get up half an hour earlier every day and teach them before breakfast. You know, 'forward bend' and all those sort of things."

Peter held the door open for Beverley. As she passed him he winked.

CHAPTER FIVE

"THERE'S a fine row going on in the servants' room," said Annie, as she drew Beverley's curtains. "Cook says she isn't going to get up early to cook your breakfast, and she's told the kitchen-maid to do it, and the kitchen-maid sauced her, and has been given notice."

Beverley sat up and reached out for her dressing-gown.

"I can't help their troubles. I'm here for the children."

"That's right." Annie flicked the curtains into place. "It's not us as'll suffer. It's Miss Winks. I wouldn't be her. When cook first heard the order she went straight to Marcelle. 'Marcelle,' she says, 'what's this rubbish I hear about this early breakfast?' 'Don't you worry, cook,' says Marcelle proud-like, 'I'll speak to "her". She'll soon settle that.'"

"What happened?" asked Beverley, pulling on her slippers.

"Marcelle came back with a flea in her ear. Muttered in a nasty way in French. She's got it in badly for you."

Beverley laughed.

"That's not likely to worry me."

Annie shook her head.

"I don't know so much. Her sort can be very sour. And she wouldn't boggle at a lie."

Beverley collected her washing things.

"This early exercising is Mrs. Cardew's orders." Annie grinned.

"So you say. But who gave her the idea. That's what I'd like to know?"

Beverley in her gym dress went into the children's sitting-room. She pulled back the table against the wall, and was just switching on the gramophone when Meggie, in shorts and a jersey, came in.

"Good morning, Meggie."

"Morning," said Meggie sourly. "The backs of my legs hurt so much after all that bending that I could hardly get into my bath this morning. I'm sure it's bad for me. I think I'm not meant to touch my toes."

"Rubbish. What tune shall I put on?"

" 'Down Among the Dead Men,' I should think. That's how I feel."

Beverley laughed.

"I'll put on the seven dwarfs' march. Go and hurry the others, there's a dear."

Meggie went out, but was back in a couple of minutes.

"David says he thinks he's got a cold coming, he better stop where he is, and Betsy says she feels weak."

Beverley's eyes twinkled.

"Betsy can't go on feeling weak for the rest of her life. I'll have a look at David."

She went to Betsy first.

"Get up, old lady. You'll have to do your exercises in your pyjamas, and dress and have your bath afterwards. Just this once I'll have your breakfast kept hot for you. If you aren't bathed and dressed by eight o'clock tomorrow you'll have a cold breakfast and do an hour's lessons in the afternoon to make up for what you miss in the morning."

"I feel awfully weak," Betsy whined. "And so would you if you'd been as sick as me."

"The doctor says you are perfectly all right now." Beverley tugged at the sheets. "Why hasn't Annie dressed you?"

"I explained I wasn't well."

Beverley cursed herself mentally for not having given Annie the order.

"Well, put on your dressing-gown and come on."

Listening to no further moans from Betsy she went in to David. He was in bed with his eyes shut. Beverley bent over him.

"It's no good pretending to be asleep. I know Annie has dressed you. If she hadn't she'd have told me."

David opened one reproachful eye.

"She has and she'll be sorry when I'm in my coffin." He made a theatrical cough.

Beverley shook her head.

"That's a bad cough. I'll send Annie in to put you to bed again."

"Well, I don't know it need be bed all day. I might feel stronger a little later on."

Beverley's eyes twinkled.

"Poor old man. Awful hour to get you up. It's rest you need. You shall have a day in bed on nothing but milk; there's nothing like it."

David sat up and put a leg out of bed.

"You're a very nasty woman. Anyone decent wouldn't try starving a person out."

Back in the children's sitting-room Beverley made a

69

face at the clock. Ten past eight—it was a slow job teaching these children to be punctual.

Because she had worked reasonably at her exercises Beverley allowed Betsy to have breakfast in her dressing-gown.

"Though only this once," she said firmly. "And Annie is to see you come down to the schoolroom at half-past nine exactly. And I've warned you what will happen if you're late another morning."

Betsy, having got her way for the moment, smiled cheerfully.

"Although I don't actually mind you, Miss Shaw, in lots of ways it was nicer being at school. Nobody to bully, bully, bully all the time."

David sighed.

"It was a lot nicer for me. I had the place to myself with you girls away."

Betsy poured some milk on her cereal.

"Nanny's boy."

David lay back in his chair and stretched his legs under the table and gave Betsy a kick.

"Ough!" Betsy yelped. "You are a hell hound."

"Betsy!" said Beverley. "It was naughty of David, but I won't have you using expressions like that."

All the children looked at her in pained surprise.

"It's Shakespeare."

"It's out of *Macbeth*."

"We're allowed to say anything if it's in Shakespeare."

"Mummy," said Betsy, "says she doesn't know what she would make speeches about if it wasn't for the awfully amusing way we misuse the bard."

Beverley took a gulp of coffee to help her control her feelings. She had forgotten where the expression came from, but even if it was *Macbeth* she did not see that made it suitable for children. But, oh dear, how difficult to train them in a house like this! What could she do if their mother told them to their faces that it was amusing?

"I do hope," said David, "Mummy isn't going to marry Sir Edward. He'd make an awfully fat stepfather."

Betsy looked up.

"And only a baronet. With all the peers about the place I hope she'll marry one of them. I'd like coronets on our notepaper."

"That Lord Malling looks awfully sloppy," said David. "I thought he'd bite Peter."

Meggie's head shot up.

"Why should he?"

Betsy paused with her spoon half-way to her mouth.

"I think Peter's got a better chance than most of them."

Meggie's eyes flashed.

"You're idiotic. Peter's much too young. Mummy wouldn't look at him."

David eyed her in surprise.

"Oh, but she is looking at him. When I went up after lessons yesterday I met him and Mummy coming down the stairs, and she hardly saw it was me she was looking at him so much."

"You're a baby," growled Meggie. "You don't understand."

"If you ask me," Beverley broke in, "you all talk too

much. I'm sure your mother wouldn't like it."

Betsy spread some toast with honey.

"You've got a very funny idea of our mother."

The telephone rang. Beverley went into the passage to answer it.

"Good morning, Joan of Arc."

"What? Who is it?"

"Peter Crewdson. You do look like Joan of Arc sometimes. I thought that perhaps today being Saturday a nature ramble for the little ones would not come amiss. If I were to bring my car at twelve might the children come to the zoo?"

"As far as I'm concerned they may, but you'd better ask Miss Winks."

"Of course I've asked Winkle, and she said, 'Oh dear me, yes, but do take Miss Shaw, one of the children might get bitten or something,' and I said, 'But of course I meant to take Miss Shaw.'"

He would have laughed if he could have seen the indignation in Beverley's eyes.

"Well, as long as that is all satisfactorily fixed up between you I've nothing to say. I and the children will be ready at twelve. Good morning."

She put down the receiver with the air of one squashing a slug.

"My goodness, that is an insufferable man," she thought. "He's always butting in over my business."

Beverley planned to be very much on her dignity, and very much the governess on the zoo expedition, but Peter was a difficult person to be dignified with, and the children were so delighted to be out with him that, without being able to help it, Beverley felt gay inside, though she hoped she did not show it.

The party started badly. The children, pleased at the combination of going out with Peter and the day being fine, came whooping down the stairs. As they reached the second floor, the door of their mother's room was flung open and Margot came out on to the landing blazing with anger.

"How dare you make that noise! Miss Shaw, what are you thinking of to allow it?"

Beverley was speechless. The children had been rather noisy, but she thought noise from a child natural, and noise from these precocious children a wholesome sound.

"I'm awfully sorry," she said at last. "They are just a little excited; they are going to the zoo with Mr. Crewdson."

Margot's face flushed, then as quickly the colour faded, leaving her unnaturally pale. Her hand on the door tightened its grip so that the knuckles stood out. Her voice dropped to almost a whisper.

"Who arranged that?"

Beverley, glancing round, was shocked to see that all three children were scared. It disgusted her that children could be afraid of their mother.

"Miss Winks," she said in a deliberately cheerful, unmoved voice.

Margot looked over her shoulder.

"Send Miss Winks to me, Marcelle."

Marcelle rang the bell and almost at once Winkle came

scuttling up the passage. Beverley nearly laughed. She looked so like the white rabbit in *Alice in Wonderland*. It would not have surprised her to have heard her say, "Oh! the Duchess, the Duchess! Oh! won't she be savage if I've kept her waiting!"

"Yes, Mrs. Cardew?" said Winkle.

"Since when have you taken upon yourself to make arrangements for my children?"

Winkle's mouth forced itself into a semblance of a smile.

"Oh, dear, I shouldn't dream of doing such a thing. If you mean this going to the zoo with Mr. Crewdson, I wasn't allowed to disturb you. You were asleep and he said, 'Don't disturb her, I won't have it.' You know how anxious he always is about you."

Margot looked slightly mollified.

"I know, but I do wish everyone would consult me. As it happens I was going to tell you to telephone Mr. Crewdson and ask him to come round here to see me."

"If you had he wouldn't have come." Peter's voice came ringing up the stairs. "Henry Dean, Leonard Boles, and Lord Malling are all coming to lunch with you and I hate the sight of the lot."

Margot's face had changed as he spoke. It was as if an iron had passed over it, smoothing away the tension.

"I wanted you to come, too. I feel nervous and unable to cope. You know how I am on a matinée day."

He ran up the stairs and came to her.

"I know, sweet. Well, go back to bed; those cads aren't due here for half an hour. Let Winkle put them off, and

74

let this be a lesson to you not to ask people to lunch when you've a matinée. You could do that, couldn't you, Winkle?"

"Oh, dear me, yes. I mean, of course I could, Mrs. Cardew, dear, if you want me to."

"And as well see that Mrs. Cardew has lunch in bed." He held up a finger at Margot. "Don't argue, you bad woman. Get back into bed. Come on, kids."

Beverley, with a feeling of distaste, saw Margot's face soften. "Good gracious," she thought as she went downstairs, "she likes being ordered about by him. How she can!"

"Shall we keep the panda to last, like saving the almond paste off one's cake, or shall we go to it straight away and stare and stare and glut ourselves with panda?" Peter inquired, turning his car into Park Lane.

"I'm not awfully sold on that panda," said David. "I like snakes."

"I want to see the panda." Betsy bounced up and down. "Last time we saw it I was photographed."

"That practically puts the panda out." Peter glanced down at her. "There's no publicity attached to this expedition."

"I like the small mammals," Meggie broke in. Peter glanced for a second over his shoulder.

"What about Miss Shaw? What does she like?"

"I shall like it all. I've never been to the zoo."

There were startled gasps from the children.

"Never been to the zoo!"

"We've been hundreds and hundreds of times."

"When we first went I was so little I was in a perambulator."

"These interesting childish reminiscences," Peter interrupted, "still do not explain why Miss Shaw has shunned the zoo."

"Well, you see I was brought up in an orphanage. It wasn't in London, and anyhow there was no money to spend on entertainments; then I trained at Melford College and that, of course, isn't in London."

"He knew you were an orphan," said Betsy. "Don't you remember the day you came when you called us toads— you said you were poor and had been brought up in an orphanage, and Peter came in and heard. Didn't you, Peter?"

"I did, Betsy, but I marvel that even a child with your hide likes to remember the occasion. I seem to recall that you outdid even your own standard of repulsiveness."

Meggie was sitting behind with Beverley; she leant forward and put her arms on the back of Peter's seat.

"Where's that man George Fane who came to the zoo with us when you took us in the summer?" Betsy nudged David and both children giggled. "Oh, shut up, you two. I suppose I can ask a question."

"Of course, dear," Betsy agreed sweetly. "I only laughed because I thought you'd know where he was."

Beverley's heart gave a thump. Whatever was this? Even as a joke Betsy's knowing tone and the giggles made her feel sick.

Meggie gave an angry jerk of her shoulders.

"Shut up."

Peter seemed not to have heard the conversation; he answered Meggie casually.

"He's on tour. They're trying out a new show."

"What a pity," said Betsy in mock sympathy. "I'm afraid Miss Meggie Cardew must put up with not seeing him."

Beverley saw red. She leant over and caught hold of Betsy by the shoulder.

"Be quiet, Betsy. I don't know in the least what you're talking about, but I don't like that smug, knowing tone of voice."

"Of course I sound knowing, because I know—"

"Be quiet. One more word and I shall ask Mr. Crewdson to stop the car and you and I'll walk home."

"And that, dear Betsy, is that," said Peter cheerfully. "And don't scowl, but have a look at the crocuses which have been planted by a generous government for our pleasure."

Beverley took a childish delight in the zoo. She hoped she was hiding her excitement at meeting all the animals she had read about under a calm governess air, but Peter was not deceived. While the children ran ahead he watched her absorbed face with a smile.

"There must be advantages in being 'little orphan Annie'—so much fun you haven't tried."

She dragged her eyes from the zebras.

"Quite a lot. People like you, with silver spoons in their mouths, don't know the half of it."

"Silver spoons! Me? I'm a working man. Didn't you know?"

"You never seem to be working."

"I see you have been harbouring the unjust illusion that I'm a rich young man about town. But I'm nothing of the sort. I'm a biological chemist. You know, I deal in the chemical constituents of these fellows." He swept his hand round the cages.

Beverley leant against the zebra's bars.

"Goodness! But when do you do it?"

He looked unhappily at her.

"Not at all at the moment. I was sent on a government survey to West Africa. And I picked up black-water fever."

She opened her eyes.

"Surely it's a miracle you're alive."

"Yes." He looked at her with interest. "You're a remarkably well-informed young woman. How do you know anything about black-water fever?"

"I don't really. But you see my father was a doctor, and about all I did inherit were his medical books. I had them at college. I often read them. Particularly the tropical diseases."

"Why?"

"I don't know." They moved on and he looked down interestedly at her eager face. "Maps have always excited me. I learn all the things about a district, the animals, and the flowers, and even the diseases. It makes me almost feel I've been there. If you've been to West Africa you must have seen zebras."

"I did."

"And panthers?"

"Did I not! It was because of a panther I got my dose of

black-water. I had to go out after one that mauled one of my bearers."

"Did you get him?"

"Yes, but I was out all night near a swamp and some mosquito handed it to me."

She gave him a quick look.

"What's it like. Is it silent? I always picture that part of Africa as feeling very big and quiet, like a cathedral, and a green, savage smell."

He nodded.

"Not far out, only your quiet is broken by the sounds of animal life. The bark and the whine, and the croaks, the crack of a rotten branch broken under an animal's pad. And then the tom-toms. Until you've heard them you don't know how they make you feel in the night. You hear a message beaten in the distance, then it comes near you, and passes down through Africa. And all our telephones, and telegrams, and modern this and that fade into nothingness. They still have us beaten, the primitive things."

Beverley gave herself a shake.

"Talking to you is bad for me. All my life I've wanted to get right away from civilization. We're so cramped and shut in. I want room for the me that's shut up to expand."

He laughed.

"It's a funny job you've chosen, then."

That got her. She flashed round at him at once.

"Not a bit. If you can't expand yourself the next best thing is to help other people to. I've got the proper job for me. I never knew children so in need of expansion as these."

He nodded.

"You've said it." They were catching up with the children; he spoke quietly. "I hope this doesn't sound cheek, but I think you're doing an awfully good job of work. Meggie's a different kid, and even Betsy's improving."

Her face lit up.

"Of course it isn't cheek. It's what I need to hear. Thank you for saying it."

That afternoon, while Margot was at the theatre, Winkle put her head round the schoolroom door.

"Can you spare me a minute, Miss Shaw?"

Beverley got up.

"Of course. Poor Meggie's struggling with a sum."

Meggie raised her eyes from the book.

"I'll say I am. You know I think it's an awful waste of time teaching me arithmetic. No actress needs to be able to add."

Winkle looked shocked.

"My dear! If only your mother knew more about figures the trouble it would save her. Since she has been managing her own theatre she has absolutely worn herself out trying to understand why they don't always pay. She thinks that every seat that is taken ought to be profit. She forgets all the expenses and author's fees and what it costs to put the production on. I often say to her, 'Just add up the running costs and then you'll see.' She does try, but, as she says, she has no head for figures. So you see, dear, how important it is."

80

Meggie propped her chin in her hands.

"What are we going to wear for that awful matinée, Winkle?"

A worried frown creased Winkle's forehead.

"My dear, if only I knew. Sir George Guggerheim is writing a prologue in blank verse, and your mother plans for the curtain to go up on you grouped round her as pieces of pottery. She thinks that because the charity is a crèche the prologue is sure to be about children, but I rang up Sir George's secretary and asked her what it was about, and she said she hadn't been given it to type yet, but she thinks it's about cows; you know, giving milk and all that sort of thing."

Meggie giggled.

"I wish Mummy would let us come on as a cow, like the sort they have in pantomimes. That would be something like."

Winkle shook her head.

"Now for goodness' sake, dear, don't say anything like that to your mother, she won't think it funny at all. I think you'll be dressed as a country group; you know, milkmaids and that kind of thing. What is worrying me is the cow. I expect if it is about cows your mother will want a model one, and she probably won't give me any notice."

"What I think—"

Beverley tapped Meggie's arithmetic book.

"And what I think is you'd better finish that sum."

Winkle led Beverley across the passage to the empty drawing-room. She carefully closed the door, and spoke in a lowered voice.

81

"If ever Mr. Crewdson, or any other of Mrs. Cardew's men friends ask the children out or come to see them, it's better if Mrs. Cardew doesn't know about it."

Beverley liked what little she knew of Winkle so she spoke more gently than she felt.

"But it's all wrong. I mean it seems deceitful. She's only got to give an order that they're not to see anyone without her permission and, of course, they won't."

Winkle pushed her glasses down her nose and stuffed her hands into her coat pockets.

"It's all so difficult. She wouldn't like that either. Theoretically, she likes her friends to be nice to the children. In fact she's hurt if they aren't."

"She didn't sound like it this morning."

"I know. This sounds disloyal, but believe me it isn't meant that way; she's a little inclined to be jealous sometimes. It wasn't really that she minded the children going out with Mr. Crewdson or anybody else; it was that they sounded so happy going down the stairs. It made her feel a little unhappy they could be enjoying things so much when she was not there."

"Well I call that disgusting."

Winkle flustered.

"Oh, my dear, if you are going to live in this house you must be more tolerant. After all, she's a genius, not an ordinary mortal like you and me."

"She's a mother, as well as a genius; she ought to be glad if her children are happy. Such a fuss about a little noise. If you ask me, her children are too fond of whispering and not nearly fond enough of healthy shouting."

82

Winkle pushed her fists down in her pockets.

"You have never seen Mrs. Cardew act; if you had, you would understand that you can't judge her by ordinary standards. I used to be a secretary to a man in the city. I hadn't much money as I have to help keep my mother and my sister's children, but every penny I had I saved to see her act. Then one day somebody told me she wanted a secretary." Her face lit up at a memory. "My dear, I couldn't believe my fortune when I was engaged. I had to keep pinching myself to be sure I was awake. Of course, there have been things to disillusion me in this house, it's only to be expected; she is, after all, human, and I came expecting to serve a goddess."

"Some goddess" was on the tip of Beverley's tongue, but she swallowed it. Instead she said gently:

"You know her, and I don't. I'll try not to let the children upset her." She hesitated. "Oh, dear, it's all so different to anything I expected. I wanted to work with the mother, not behind her back."

Winkle, very awkwardly, as though the gesture were foreign to her, pulled one hand out of her pocket and laid it on Beverley's arm.

"It's because of the difficulties in this house that you are so very much needed. Do try and stop."

In the days that followed, Beverley had to remind herself quite often of that conversation with Winkle, for Peter came almost daily to the nursery, and though she hoped she was wrong, she was convinced that neither he nor the children ever mentioned the visits to Margot. She felt particularly awkward about his visits because she found she was looking forward to them. At tea-time (which was his usual calling hour, for Margot went to bed in the afternoons when she had not got a matinée and never got up until half-past five) she caught herself straining her ears for the sound of footsteps. As the door opened and she heard his gay voice greeting the children, it was as if some part of her mind which had been keyed up, relaxed. Sometimes he had tea with them, sometimes he was too late for that and taught the children card games or told them stories of wild animals, but no matter what he was doing, he always had quite a lot to say to her in the laughing, bantering tone he kept especially for her. Beverley, pouring out the tea, or sewing or correcting exercise books by the fire, was careful to treat his visits with an appearance of stony disinterest; too well she knew the sharpness of the children's eyes.

Even though she enjoyed his visits, Beverley could not get over feeling ashamed by them, a feeling which was accentuated by annoyance with herself for enjoying them. Then, one afternoon, all her dislike of the situation was crystallized. Peter had been to tea with the children and had stayed on to teach them a card trick. He had just asked David to draw any card he liked from the pack when the door opened and Winkle put her head into the room.

"She's getting up, Mr. Crewdson."

Peter laid down the pack on the table.

"That is the end of the children's hour for tonight." He got up. " I've got to go down to your mother."

Beverley felt her cheeks flaming

"Why don't the children take the cards downstairs and get you to show them the rest of the trick in the drawing-room?"

The three children looked awkward, but Peter seemed merely amused.

"If you look so like Joan of Arc, I shall buy you a white charger."

"Joan of Arc didn't look a bit like Miss Shaw," said Meggie.

Peter did not take his eyes off Beverley.

"Well, she's my idea of how she looked." He gave Beverley an amused twinkle. "Do you particularly wish the children to finish the card trick?"

She flung up her chin.

"Yes."

He raised his eyebrows.

"Why?"

She looked at him furiously. How frightfully mean of him, she thought, to ask "why" like that. He knew perfectly well she couldn't explain in front of the children.

"Because—"

He grinned.

"Don't bother." He came across the room and gently laid the pack on her knee. "If you want them taken to the drawing-room, I'm not stopping you. I like seeing what people's principles are worth."

"I say, are you going to bring the cards down?" Meggie asked anxiously as the door closed.

Betsy hopped across the room.

85

"What did Peter mean about your principals? Principals are head mistresses; we had them at our schools."

Beverley calmly put the cards on the mantelpiece.

"That's the p-a-l-s kind; there are as well p-l-e-s. Those are the kind he was talking about. Now run along and get changed."

Meggie loitered, pretending to put away a book.

"I don't think Mummy knew Peter had been up here to tea," she said awkwardly.

Beverley nodded.

"That's what Mr. Crewdson meant. I don't think your mother minds him or anyone else coming to tea with you, but I'd rather she always knew."

Meggie stood on one leg.

"Sometimes Mummy is angry about things she doesn't mind."

Beverley smiled.

"There's no need to look so worried. Your mother, like all very brilliant people, is inclined to get upset easily. But however easily she is upset I can't have Peter sneaking in and out of the schoolroom as if you people had an infectious illness. I like things done in the open."

Meggie slid one foot along the carpet.

"You're going to take down those cards and tell her?"

"Yes. Unless you'll do it for me. You needn't take the cards down; just let your mother know naturally. Say he was here to tea; she won't mind. Why should she?"

Meggie slid her foot on another inch or two, then she looked up.

"Very well, I'll do it."

"Promise?"

"Yes."

The children, Beverley was relieved to notice, came up no earlier than usual, and looking perfectly cheerful.

"Mummy has been sent a perfectly gorgeous play to read," said David. "She strangles her husband and buries him under some floor boards, and when people come to look for him she thinks she hears him moving, and she goes madder and madder until just as the curtain falls she starts to scratch up the boards with her nails."

"Next Saturday we are to go to the matinée, and you're coming too. Mummy says she can't have somebody in the house who has never seen her act, and Meggie an' me can wear our white fur coats and hats."

"And won't the little Miss Cardews look ducks!" said David.

In the argument between Betsy and David which followed this bit of rudeness, Beverley looked across at Meggie.

"Did you tell your mother what you promised?" Meggie hunched her shoulders.

"Of course. What d'you think?"

Beverley felt as if a window had been opened in a hot room. How nice to feel that nothing underhand was going on. She took a sudden pleasure in the coming matinée. If Mrs. Cardew had said they were to go, then she certainly was not cross about anything.

While she and Meggie were at supper, Beverley asked about the plot of Margot's play, but Meggie was in a particularly unresponsive mood; she only gave angry shakes of her shoulders, muttering:

"I don't know. Like any other play, I suppose."

She picked and turned over her fish, and left most of her fruit salad. Beverley looked at her anxiously, hoping she was not ill. Just as they were finishing the meal, the door opened a crack and round came Peter's face. He shook his head at Beverley.

"You've let me down, Joan of Arc. I'd have staked my life you'd have stood by a principle."

"But—" Beverley looked at Meggie's crimson cheeks and her voice tailed away.

Peter looked from one to the other of them, then he withdrew his head, saying, "This time it vanished quite slowly, beginning with the end of its tail, and ending with the grin."

There was dead silence in the room as the door shut. Meggie, scarlet to the ears, sat staring at her hands, then, suddenly, she put her head on the table and burst into a flood of tears.

Beverley got up and knelt beside her, and, hardly daring to hope she would not be repulsed, drew the child's head on to her shoulder. To her amazement, Meggie dragged her arms free and put them around her.

"I am so sorry. I didn't mean to tell a lie. I hate telling one to you."

"Well, why did you?"

"She frightens me so. She always has. I adore her, but when she's angry, she looks wicked and I can't bear it."

Beverley held the child closer.

"Why didn't you tell me that, darling? I would have

88

talked to your mother. You know that."

"No. I did mean to. I would rather it was me instead of you. I'm so afraid if she gets angry with you she'll send you away."

Beverley gently stroked Meggie's head.

"You mean you want me to stay?"

She was startled at the passion in the child's reply. "Of course I do. I love you."

CHAPTER SIX

HAVING opened her heart, Meggie seemed like a plant lifting up its leaves at the first rain after a drought. Beverley had told Sarah she was like a frostbitten rose, and daily she saw how true her simile had been. It seemed as if the child had been wrapped in layer after layer of repression, and with it peeling from her the real Meggie emerged. She even seemed in better health, from having been sallow cheeked, a faint flush made her twice as good looking. To Beverley, enchanted though she was by the change, she presented difficulties. It was not any part of her educational belief that her pupils' improvement should hang on herself. At the same time she dare not repel Meggie's advances. It was plain she was starved for friendship and understanding, and was not yet sufficiently on her own feet to be taught not to depend for these things on any one person. One of the worst features of Meggie's blossoming affection was that her mother's disease of jealousy began to show in her. Having, as it were, discovered Beverley, she wanted her all to herself. The slightest signs of fondness given her by the other two were received with glowers, glowers which did not miss the ever watchful Betsy, who, out of sheer cussedness, at once began hugging and kissing Beverley, and gloating over Meggie's frowns.

To Beverley's annoyance the one person who grasped the situation was Peter. The day after Meggie's confession she had a note from him.

"MY DEAR JOAN OF ARC,

I am sorry I misjudged you even for a second. To put your trembling conscience at rest I took over the faithless Meggie's job. It all passed off very nicely.

Yours,

P.C."

He was up playing with the children the next day and made no reference to his note, only as he was leaving he said, apparently to them all but actually with a twinkling eye fixed on Beverley:

"Well, you must change, and I must go down to your mother. She says she is sure too much of you little horrors is bad for me."

It was not until a week later that he mentioned Meggie. The children were at their dancing class; Annie had taken them because Beverley had a good deal of work to arrange and correct. She was at the table in the children's sitting-room with a pile of books in front of her when Peter looked in.

"Hullo. Busy?"

"Yes."

He shut the door and sat on the table.

"All the same I shall interrupt you." He fiddled with a work-chart she was ruling. "Difficult about young Meggie."

She had no false pride with him now.

"It's difficult to know what to do. You see I don't feel my position is as secure as all that. Meggie's such a funny child; I don't want to let her get fond of me and then

91

perhaps have to leave her. She'd be more shut in on herself than ever."

He picked up her ruler and balanced it on one of his fingers.

"You have grasped, I suppose, that if her mother felt you or anyone were coming first with her children it would be o-u-t."

"I have, though mind you I think it's awful to be so egotistical."

He smiled.

"She's an artist; you can't judge them by ordinary standards. Now there's no repression about her; she's one of those fully expanded people you were talking about."

It was on the tip of Beverley's tongue to say, "If that's expansion, I don't want it," but she bit it back. She leant her chin on her hands.

"Well, the children are repressed. They don't seem so always, but they are. They're like plants trained to climb a certain way." Her eyes twinkled. "I often feel as though I'd sneaked into a garden and were snipping down all the bits of bass which tie up the branches of the plants, and pulling out the nails which hold them to the walls."

He played with a ruler.

"Grand. But don't be too violent. It would be awfully bad luck on the kids if you went now."

She beamed.

"You've no idea how nice it makes me feel when you say things like that. I feel all purry like a cat."

He shook his head at her.

"And you should try and appreciate Mrs. Cardew. She's

a grand person in lots of ways."

Beverley hoped her face did not show what she thought. She supposed Peter was in love with Margot, and it seemed to her a pity. Why did his sort of person, who belonged to forests and spaces, want to go falling in love with an actress years older than himself? Margot might be a splendid actress—she had not had a chance to judge that yet, and in any case knew nothing about acting—but she did know something about bringing up children, and in her opinion Margot was an awful mother.

"I expect it's just that I don't understand her type," she said, trying to sound nice. "I'm going to see her act on Saturday afternoon, and after that I expect I shall feel quite different about her."

He gave her the same rather tender smile, then he picked up her work-chart.

"Monday," he read. "7.30—get up. 8—exercises. 8.30—breakfast. Meggie, 9.30—French exercise. 10—arithmetic (alone)." He grinned. "Poor Meggie, arithmetic is bad enough without solitary confinement thrown in." He went back to the chart. " 10.30—history essay. 11—break for milk. 11.15—map-drawing. 12—walk. 2.30—German. 3—algebra. 3.30—Latin. 4—geography. Mercy, what a day."

"You've no idea what it's like." Beverley took the chart from him. "Think of their ages. You don't know how I have to squeeze things in. I'm using this room now for Meggie in the mornings. You see while she's doing a French exercise Betsy is doing French conversation. Well, you can't have the two things going on in the same room."

"What about David?"

"He's doing his drawing. He's rather good. I'm working them all for the Royal Drawing Society's examinations."

"What happens to the other two while Meggie is doing her solitary arithmetic?"

"They do arithmetic, too. David's just beginning to add and Betsy doesn't know much more. Then after that I take David for a reading lesson and I send Betsy up to Meggie to write a history essay. I take all of them together for history on Tuesdays and Fridays."

"I'm glad to see the poor little dears are allowed a glass of milk, anyway."

Beverley laughed.

"The best tuberculin-tested, and two biscuits. A different kind each day so that they won't get tired of any one sort."

He had another look at the chart.

"Then you teach Betsy and David to write."

"That's right. At twelve we go out until twenty past one. We walk in Hyde Park. It's nice having the parks so near."

"What happens to David and Betsy while Meggie does her German and Latin and all the rest of it?"

"They go out with Annie, the maid. I choose different places for them to look at. You know, bits of old London and houses where interesting people have lived."

"Doesn't Meggie ever see the gorgeous sights of the town?"

She laughed.

"Every Saturday we go an expedition. At this time of

the year it's the museums and picture galleries, but directly the weather is better I plan to take them by boat to Hampton Court and round the docks, and to the Tower. Such a lot of London history is mixed up with the Thames I want them to go to all the historical places on its banks, and really know it well."

He raised his eyebrows at the chart.

"Extraordinary! I see tea at 4.45, and that they change and go down to the drawing-room, but it doesn't say 5.15—Uncle Peter, and I think it should."

She shook her head.

"This is a serious chart."

"I can see it is." He turned over the pile of papers. "A different page for every day."

Beverley sighed.

"It all looks so lovely, but it never works out like that. I don't suppose there's one day when we really do everything I've put down. Of course, I've put down the outside extras, their dancing classes, and elocution classes, but it's the other things we have to fit in. For instance, both the girls have to go to the hairdresser every week."

"No! I thought kids of that age had it washed at home."

"I wish they did; it wastes an awful lot of time. I never knew such looked-after hair. Annie has to brush each of their heads for twenty minutes every evening. Then there's dressmakers. They go to a dressmaker in Hanover Square and there hardly seems to be a day when one of them hasn't to go for a fitting, or David to his tailor's. Just now they are having dresses made for that charity matinee. They are a group of pottery and they take a lot of

95

fitting, and soon they're to go for rehearsals of the tableau or whatever they are. Then there're photographs. They've been to photographers twice already since I've been here."

He chuckled.

"Poor Joan of Arc. It's a hard life."

She looked up at him, flushing.

"I'm just as keen on bringing up children as you are on your biochemistry. You know all about the chemicals that make an animal. I've studied the slugs and snails and puppy dogs' tails, and the sugar and spice that make a child. It's my job and I'm going to do it well. So don't laugh at me."

"Laugh!" He laid a hand over hers. "I've never laughed yet at the sight of somebody getting down to a good job of work."

Beverley did not go straight back to her books. Instead, she stared at the hand he had held, her heart beating.

"Funny," she thought, "everything seems interesting when he's in the room, and duller when he's away."

Beverley was keyed up with excitement when they went to the theatre on Saturday. Peter and Winkle and the children had given her the feeling that once she had seen Margot act she would find her easy to understand.

She had only been to the theatre once or twice and then she had sat in the pit. Going with Margot's children made theatres seem quite different places. No getting there by bus or tube, no waiting in the queue, no eating an indigestible meal out of a bag. They had luncheon a little earlier, the car came for them at two, they swept up to the front of the theatre where a smiling saluting commissionaire addressed by the children as "Fred" opened the door and helped them out. In the foyer the manager was waiting; he beamed at the children and led the way to the stage box where four programmes and a box of chocolates were waiting for them.

Beverley was overcome at the grandeur of everything, and cowered into a corner when she saw that the children had been recognized by quite a lot of the audience who examined them through opera glasses and nudged each other.

The children were evidently so accustomed to publicity that they were not embarrassed. Meggie, without even glancing at the audience, opened her coat and settled down to read the magazine page on the programme. David hung over the box and waved to the orchestra; as the orchestra were in the middle of a number they had difficulty in acknowledging that they had seen him, but he was satisfied.

"You see that fat man, he's the first violin," he said to Beverley. "His little boy, who's the same age as me, nearly died when his appendix burst. I asked if I could see the appendix when it came out, but I never did."

Betsy gave Meggie a nudge.

"I do think you might look at the people a bit, they like to know we're here."

Meggie glanced up and watched Betsy beaming at the programme girls.

"They aren't likely to miss us with you in the theatre."

Betsy took off her white fur hat and shook out her curls.

"I think it's our duty as Mummy's children to make ourselves pleasant." She leant over for the box of chocolates. "Bags I the ribbon."

"You'll make yourself awfully pleasant if you eat too many chocolates and are sick on the big drum," said David.

Beverley took the chocolates from Betsy.

"No one is going to eat chocolates just yet. You can all have one in the interval."

Betsy flushed.

"They were given to us, not to you. People don't give chocolates to governesses."

Meggie's head rose, her eyes flashing.

"You are a beast, Betsy."

Beverley laid a hand on Meggie's knee.

"This is the first time I've seen your mother act; don't spoil it for me by quarrelling."

Neither Betsy nor Meggie showed much sign of listening to her appeal, but at that moment the theatre lights dimmed and the curtains began to rise.

Beverley had supposed that she would only be able to give half her attention to the stage and half to keeping the children quiet, but there she misjudged children born of the theatre. The play was above their heads and they had seen it before, but from the second the curtain rose they became like statuary, intent and eager, taking in every word and gesture, but without a fidget amongst them.

The play was rather a creaking affair. The scene was laid in a manufacturing town. The old people had made money, called by the father "brass". Wealth as used by them all sat uncomfortably on them. The sons and daughters and their wives and husbands were a discontented lot, belonging neither to the class to which their money had carried them, nor to their own people from which their money separated them. All the family were gathered to meet the youngest boy's, Alan's, wife. He had done what none of them had managed, he had married into the class which was accustomed to money. Sybil was the daughter of an Earl, and her coming was awaited by all the family with ill-disguised nervousness. Margot, of course, played Sybil.

Margot hated matinées; lot of sleepy old crows she always called the audience. But that day as she came on the stage she had one of her flashes; she ceased to be Margot Dale and was the sensitive Sybil who, in desperation, had sold herself to a man she did not love. The cast, lighting up as actors always do to first-class playing, thought, "It must be because her children are in front." But they were wrong. Margot, waiting to come on, had peered through a hole in a flat at the children, but it was on Beverley her eyes had stayed. The effects had just made the sound of what was supposed to be her and Alan's car off stage. All the audience were gluing their eyes on the door for her entrance; most of them were looking expectant, but not Beverley—on her face was written scepticism. "Now let's see this great acting I've heard so much about. I bet they've exaggerated." It was just the touch Margot needed. She shook off her lethargy like a cloak, and it was a great actress at her greatest who came on to the stage.

Beverley lost herself. She had the same exhilarated feeling you can get when you lose your feet bathing and are swept up and taken command of by a great wave. On she went, over and over, with spray in her eyes, to be thrown up breathless on the shore as the curtain dropped.

Meggie turned to her with sparkling eyes.

"Isn't Mother marvellous?"

Even Margot's ego would have been satisfied if she could have heard the fervour with which Beverley answered.

It was all Beverley could do to bring herself back to the box and the children, and to supervise their tea which the management sent. All she could do to stop them telling her the story. She did not want to hear it from them, she wanted to live it with their mother.

It seemed to her no time before the curtain was dropping for the last time. She would have sat clapping until midnight if the orchestra had not forced her to her feet playing "God Save the King".

Betsy nudged her, holding out her white fur coat.

"Please help me on. We're going round to see Mummy now."

It had never struck Beverley that there was only a simple door between the audience and the actors. The pass door was inside their box. Feeling like somebody in a fairy story she found herself on the other side of the iron door, in a world of running stage hands, hanging ropes, and suddenly dimmed lights.

"Is that my babies?" Margot called when David knocked on her door.

There was the sound of shuffling feet and the door opened and a head poked out.

"It's them, right enough. Come in, dears."

Mrs. Brown, Margot's dresser, had dressed her since she first had a dressing-room to herself. And that, as she always said, "Is more years than we care to remember." Margot never really liked Mrs. Brown, who was strict with her and stood for no nonsense.

"I stood for no nonsense from Brown," she told Margot at the beginning of her time with her, "and any woman who could keep Brown in his place knew something."

She evidently had learnt something from her late husband for her effect on Margot was renowned. Many times had producers and managers gone to Mrs. Brown when all normal methods of persuasion had failed, and she usually got things done.

"Leave it to me," she would say. "She's just actin' up. I'll soon see to that."

The truth was that Margot was afraid of Mrs. Brown. Partly because she was the one person who was never scared of her, and partly because she was superstitious, and so would not open in a show until she was in the theatre. Once, years before, Mrs. Brown had been taken with influenza before a first night, and was too weak to act as dresser, but Margot had sent a car for her, and from a sofa she had supervised the work of a temporary dresser, and Margot had gone on the stage perfectly happy because her mascot was in the theatre.

Margot, in a dressing-gown was taking off her make-up.

"Oh, Mummy, you were good today," said Meggie.

"Mummy's always good," said Betsy.

"We have our ups and downs," Mrs. Brown broke in. "This afternoon was one of our ups."

David wandered round the dressing-room.

"I thought you were awfully good, but I never did like this play awfully. I'll be glad when the bookings drop and you rehearse that new one where you go mad."

Beverley was standing just inside the door. Margot looked at her.

"And Miss Shaw. What did she think?"

Beverley struggled for the right words.

"I never knew acting could be like that."

Margot was used to endless praise, but the note of admiration satisfied her. She looked at Beverley with new eyes. She had scarcely thought of her since she came to the house, except the time when she had allowed the children to make a noise on the stairs, and vaguely when Peter had told her he usually played cards with the children after their tea. There seemed now more to her than she had imagined. A person who was capable of appreciating good acting could not be entirely negligible, and negligible was the word that had come to her mind when she considered her in relation to Peter.

"I'm so glad you enjoyed it," she said. "You shall come to the first night of my next play, or the dress rehearsal. We shall see. David, don't fidget with Mummy's flowers. Betsy, my precious, put down that hare's foot, those cheeks don't need rouging."

"You keep off the paint and powder, Miss Betsy," Mrs. Brown put in. "It's been the downfall of more than one."

102

David looked up from a large gilt basket of azaleas he was examining.

"Why should painting your face make you fall?"

Mrs. Brown shook her head at him.

"Ah, it's grand to be innocent. You'll grow up fast enough, young man."

"Betsy, don't fidget with Mummy's things." Margot, exhausted by the afternoon's performance, looked at Beverley. "Take them away, Miss Shaw. Nobody 'oves her babies more than I do, but poor Mummy has to act again tonight. Good-bye, little darlings. Good-bye."

Betsy and David came home in a rampageous mood. Beverley was sorry to quell them as she thought a little natural rampageousness would not hurt, but it was too near bed-time to have them overexcited. But quelling was one thing and having any result quite another.

"Let's pretend we are the king and queen, David," Betsy suggested. "I'll bow to all the people and you'll salute."

Owing to David and Betsy being small this game was harmless as they scarcely showed to the passersby, but after a bit Betsy noticed they were not attracting the attention she had hoped. First she stood up, and then began knocking on the windows, and David copied her.

"Sit down, both of you," said Beverley.

"Sit down, David," Betsy mimicked, bowing to an astonished old gentleman.

David grinned over his shoulder.

"Oh, I gave that lady a lovely salute."

Beverley pulled them on to their seats.

"I don't want to be cross; we've had a lovely afternoon,

but that game is finished."

Betsy struggled free and gave a bow and a wave of the hand to a tradesboy, who responded by whistling through his fingers.

"You may have finished, but me and David haven't."

"David and I haven't," Beverley corrected. "And as a matter of fact you have, because I'm going to stop the car and you and David and I are going to walk home."

Betsy turned on her a face of rage.

"You are the most annoying woman. I was just having fun. And you know I wouldn't walk home. You just think out ways to be savage."

"Oh, shut up," Meggie growled. "I can't think how Miss Shaw can bear you."

"I'm sure you can't, dear," Betsy agreed. "Darling, darling, Miss Shaw." She snuggled into Beverley and rubbed her cheek on her sleeve. "I adore you, Miss Shaw."

Beverley laughed and pushed her away.

"You are a little silly, aren't you? What would you and David like for supper?"

"Caviare," David suggested.

"No." Betsy made a face. "Even thinking of that makes me feel very odd. I think I'd like a slice of pineapple and cream."

Beverley pretended to consider.

"Of course those are both very good suggestions for nursery supper, but I myself was going to limit the choice to a cereal, or Marmite, or a milk-food and biscuits."

The discussion as to what they should eat was still at its height when they reached Way Street. The front door was no sooner open than Betsy and David ran screaming up the stairs.

"Annie, we want sardines and cream-cheese for supper. Annie, we want pêche Melbas."

As Beverley reached the top of the stairs Annie gave a grin.

"Proper above themselves. What shall I give them for supper?"

Beverley laughed.

"Something soothing."

"Bread and milk, then." Annie stepped down the stairs. "After a treat my mother always gave us bread and milk. Soothes the stomach, she said, and makes any child act sensible."

"I'm a ferret," said Betsy, crawling up the passage. "I'm ferreting my way in everywhere."

"Well, you better be quick." Beverley turned towards her room. "Annie won't be long bringing your supper."

David was sitting cross-legged outside her door.

"Don't interrupt me," he said without looking up. "I'm Gandhi meditating."

She stepped round him carefully.

"A very excellent thing to be. You see how soon you can meditate yourself into feeling like bed."

Beverley had just got her hat off when she was startled by a piercing scream.

"You beast. You beast. Put them back." Beverley, recognizing Meggie's voice, flew to her room. Horrified, she found her with both hands on Betsy's shoulders shaking the child to and fro and banging her head on the door. "You cad. You beast. You lily-livered loon. I hate you. I hate you."

"Meggie!" Beverley dragged her off Betsy. "How dare you!"

Meggie, with tears streaming down her face, stamped her foot.

"Of course I dare. I wish I'd killed her. She's loathsome. A paul-pry."

Beverley turned to Betsy.

"Betsy, what have you found?"

A most unpleasant smile curled Betsy's lips.

"I was a ferret. Ask her what I found under her mattress."

"You only played being a ferret to have an excuse to look under my mattress," sobbed Meggie.

"You look," said Betsy, "then you'll see why she tried to kill me."

Beverley fixed Betsy with her eye.

"Did you pretend to be a ferret just to have an excuse to look under her bed?"

Betsy scrubbed at the carpet with her toe.

"Well, as a matter of fact, I did. I thought——"

"I have not the faintest interest in what you thought. Go to your bedroom and start getting undressed. I'll come and talk to you presently."

"But——"

Beverley never took her eyes off the child's face.

"Go on."

Left alone she looked at the sobbing Meggie.

"I'll send your supper to you in bed. No matter what

106

Betsy has done you have behaved abominably and I'm disgusted. I do dislike that sort of lack of self-control." Her voice softened. "As for what she did or did not find under your mattress you can tell me or not as you like. I shall never ask. I'll be in presently to say good night."

In the passage David shook his head at her gloomily.

"You shouldn't have stopped them. There's a lot of pleasure to be had out of a murder."

She laughed.

"You horrid child. I hear Annie on the stairs. I'll have supper in the sitting-room with you while she puts Betsy to bed."

Half an hour later she went to Betsy's room. Betsy sat up as the door opened.

"I'm not a bit sorry. I consider I was perfectly right. A child that age has no business with—"

Beverley sat down on the edge of Betsy's bed.

"I don't know what you found under the mattress and you are not going to tell me."

"Is Meggie going to?"

"Probably." Beverley looked at the child. "I wonder why you do and say such horrid things?"

Betsy considered the question.

"I shall probably grow up very interesting. Children who are bad usually do."

Beverley restrained a smile.

"But yours seems to me such a nasty kind of badness. The sort that makes everybody dislike you."

"Mummy doesn't dislike me."

"Of course not, but I think that you could grow up an

amusing and entertaining person, instead of which you'll grow up the sort of person people describe as a cat."

Betsy looked thoughtful.

"You know I think there's two me's. As a matter of fact, I didn't be a ferret to look in Meggie's bed, but when I was a ferret I thought of it. Well, you must blame the ferret, not me."

Beverley's eyes twinkled.

"Can you think of a nice person or animal you could be for a day or two, an obliging creature who said nice things?"

"I could be a panda. I'd be a little proud, because pandas are, but I'd be nice."

"Would you start by being a panda in the morning?"

"I'd have to wear white or I wouldn't feel like one."

Beverley remembered all she had been taught about bribing children, but this family were teaching her things that came in no college course.

"Very well."

"Can I wear my white fur coat or my white cloth one when I go out?"

"Very well. But if the panda isn't all I think a panda should be, off will come the white, and I shall put you in overalls in the house, and a mackintosh out of doors."

Betsy smiled seraphically.

"Miss Betsy Cardew disappears and Miss Panda takes her place."

Beverley got up and stooped to kiss her.

"Well, see she does."

Unexpectedly Betsy threw her arms round her neck.

"You don't dislike me, do you?"

"Very often."

Betsy hugged her.

"You won't tomorrow."

Meggie was lying with her face to the wall when Beverley went in. She sprang up and held out her hand.

"I'm awfully sorry."

Beverley put her arm round her.

"It's all over, but for your own sake never let it happen again. An uncontrolled person is a nuisance in the world." She gave her a kiss. "Now don't think any more about it tonight, but go to sleep."

Meggie dived under her pillow and brought out an envelope and pushed it into Beverley's hands.

"There it is. That's what she found."

With the door shut Beverley opened the envelope at the schoolroom table. There was a photograph of a young man with "To my friend Meggie, from George Fane" written on the corner. There were three snaps of the same young man with the three children at the zoo. There was a letter very much read and folded. It said:

"DEAR LITTLE MEGGIE,

Thank you so much for your sweet letter. I am glad you liked me so much in the part.

Your affectionate friend,

GEORGE FANE."

There were two or three ribbons off chocolate-boxes with sticking plaster on each and on the plaster was written, "Given by him," and then a date.

Beverley turned over the comic little collection.

The words of a woman psychologist rang in her ears. "Youthful crazes and crushes for people want treating with the utmost care. The young girl who finds something to love usually does so because she is thwarted in some way. If it is necessary to persuade her away from the object of her affection, the subject must be broached with extreme delicacy or irreparable harm may be done."

Beverley put the collection back in its envelope. Poor little Meggie, hero-worshipping this young man who probably knew nothing about it, and would be shocked if he did. What ought she to do? If she could have ignored the subject it would probably die a natural death. But she couldn't ignore it. A little girl of twelve hugging photographs and a letter was silly and, if encouraged, vulgar. Unconsciously she dropped her head on her hands and closed her eyes.

"Dear God, I feel so incompetent. Show me the right way to handle this."

CHAPTER SEVEN

BEVERLEY woke with a feeling of thankfulness that it was Sunday. Nanny, determined that the children should be brought up with religious teaching, had taken them to a children's service on Sunday afternoons. Somehow, although Margot seldom went to church herself, except for a memorial service or a wedding, it was a custom of which she vaguely approved and had allowed to stand. Beverley had, of course, carried on with the tradition; one Sunday she took the children, and the next Annie, according to which was off duty. This was Annie's Sunday on and Beverley gave a thankful sigh as she wriggled more comfortably into bed. Although she was glad she had got the children up earlier, and glad they were doing exercises, she was very glad of her extra hour on Sundays.

She did not officially start her half-day until after lunch, but she and Annie had a working arrangement that on their half-Sundays the other one took the children for their walk.

"And very glad I am," thought Beverley, "with Betsy being a panda and my not knowing yet what I want to say to Meggie, it'll be a God-send. I'll go to church this morning, that might help, and perhaps Sarah will give me an idea this afternoon."

There was a knock on her door. Annie came in.

"Brought you a cup of tea, seeing it's Sunday. Is that right what Betsy says—that she's to get up all in white?"

Beverley sipped the tea gratefully.

"How nice of you, Annie. Yes. She says she can behave better if she pretends to be a panda. She's going to be one for a day or two."

Annie drew back the curtains.

"Hope I don't have her acting like a panda in the park when I take them out. Proper show she makes of herself, Miss Betsy does."

"Well, she's only to wear her white things as long as she's good. If she makes more of a show of herself than you think reasonable, warn her it means a pinafore and a mackintosh."

Annie laughed.

"That ought to settle her. Miss Vain she is and no mistake. Meggie's got a headache. Looks properly washed out. I told her to stop where she was."

"Oh dear, that must be the upset last night. The doctor told me she was easily overstrained."

"That's right. That Marcelle was nosing at supper last night. 'That Miss Shaw doesn't seem to keep the children very quiet,' she said, nasty like. 'Well,' I said, taking her up quick, 'that's seeing their mother do her acting. Put them properly above themselves it has.' 'If you ask me, it's overtired they are,' Marcelle says, looking at cook in a very meaning way. 'No wonder,' says cook. 'Cruelty, I call it, dragging the little innocents out of their beds at half-past seven.' For she doesn't like the new kitchen-maid and blames it on you. 'I think I shall tell my lady about the screaming,' Marcelle says, giving me a nasty look. 'It isn't what she'd like at all, it isn't.' "

Beverley looked anxious.

112

"She doesn't know what it was about, does she?"

Annie tapped her nose with her forefinger.

"Not her. Mind you, I don't know properly what was up myself. Miss Betsy talked about some things of Miss Meggie's when I was undressing her, but I didn't listen."

"Good," Beverley said. "Just a storm in a tea-cup; the least anybody says about it the better." She got out of bed and put on her dressing-gown. "I'll go along and have a look at Meggie."

Meggie was lying with her sheet over her face to keep out the light. She peered out as Beverley came in and tried to sit up. Beverley was shocked at her appearance. Her face was yellow, her lips almost colourless, and her eyes the size of saucers with dark lines half down her cheeks. Beverley leant over her.

"Don't try and sit up, darling. What is it? A headache?"

"Partly, and a pain here." She hugged her diaphragm.

"Do you feel sick?"

Meggie's eyes filled with tears.

"Not exactly. I feel awful everywhere."

Beverley stroked the hair off the child's forehead.

"Poor old lady. I'll draw the curtains to keep the light off your eyes, and bring you a hot-water bottle. What did Nanny do for you when you were like this?"

"Oh, just aspirins. It passes off."

Beverley sought out Annie.

"I think it's nervous exhaustion, and as a result of it, nervous indigestion."

Annie was impressed.

"My, don't you know a lot."

"We had a good course on children's ailments at my college. I'm going to try dosing her with ginger and bicarbonate in boiling water for the indigestion, and aspirins for the headache. We'll repeat the ginger and bicarbonate in an hour, and if she isn't fit enough by then to face some breakfast, I shall send for the doctor."

After the second dose of the indigestion mixture Meggie asked for coffee and toast. Beverley gave it to her and, since her headache was better, a book to read, and told her to stop where she was until lunchtime. Then she took herself into the children's sitting-room. She was sorry to have missed church, but she couldn't leave Meggie. Laughing, she watched from the window Betsy and David and Annie start off for their walk. Betsy, complete in the ermine outfit she had worn yesterday, prancing and posing up the street. However, according to her lights she had been good that morning, so Beverley was able to watch her with tolerance.

"Hullo. So you've sent your two little dears out without you."

Beverley swung round to Peter.

"What are you doing up here?"

"I came to see Mrs. Cardew. We're going out of town for lunch. But she's still in her bath."

"If you came to see Meggie, I think you'd better not. I want to keep her quiet a bit longer."

"What's up with her?"

"Nervous attack. I believe she's subject to them."

"They're all too highly strung to live. What set her off?"

Beverley fidgeted with the curtain.

"We went to see Mrs. Cardew's matinée yesterday. It could have been that."

He laughed.

"You ought never to lie. You are the most transparent liar."

Beverley wandered over to the table, playing for time. Peter was this man George Fane's friend—Meggie had asked about him that day on the way to the zoo. On the other hand it was Meggie's silly little secret. It seemed hardly fair to discuss it. Yet if anyone understood Meggie, he seemed to.

"All right," he said. "Don't tell me. I can see it in your face when you're saying, 'Damn the fellow. He's always butting in.' "

She raised her chin.

"As a matter of fact, this time I wasn't thinking that. Though I often do. I was wondering whether I'd tell you." She sat down. "I think I will. What's your friend George Fane like?"

He felt in his pocket and took out a cigarette-case.

"He doesn't know Meggie's fond of him, if that's what you mean. He looks upon her as a small child."

"So she is."

He passed her his cigarette-case.

"Smoke?" She shook her head. "This is a bit of a forcing house. They're too knowledgeable, this trio."

"Lots of girls keep photographs of actors and film-stars."

"Yes." He looked at her with friendly eyes. "Then why do you mind?"

She told him what had happened the night before.

"Betsy looked so sly over the whole thing, and Meggie losing her temper like that, I feel as if it all needs a spring-clean."

"What are you going to do?"

"I think I'll have to have a talk with Mrs. Cardew."

He looked startled.

"For heaven's sake don't. She likes that sort of thing. She'll tell everybody, and make Meggie wretched and infuriate George."

"Well, what would you do?"

"Oh, shove the things back at her, and let her see you don't care one way or the other, but think it's a bit silly."

She looked doubtful.

"It's the secrecy, and Betsy's face."

He put a hand on her arm.

"Aren't you fussing too much? She's rather friendless, poor kid. A little doting on George won't hurt her."

The door behind them creaked. They both turned quickly, but no one was there. Puzzled, Peter got up and opened it. Marcelle was standing outside.

"What on earth are you doing?" he asked.

She gave the two of them a queer smile.

"I was just goin' to knock to know if you was there. Mrs. Cardew wish you to come down. She say she is ready."

"All right. I'll follow you."

He waited until Marcelle was out of hearing, then he made a face at Beverley.

"I believe she looked in."

"Well, suppose she did. What harm was there?"

"Absolutely none, but you don't know Marcelle."

As Peter reached the bottom of the stairs Marcelle was waiting.

"Hullo," he said. "What do you want?"

She pursed her lips and shrugged her shoulders.

"Miss Shaw is new to the 'ouse. She does not know how it would be if Madame knew you pay her a little visit."

"Good Lord, woman, what a mind you've got. I was only talking about the children."

Her lips twisted at the corners.

"Your hand is on her arm."

He looked at her with loathing.

"You are an unpleasant piece of work. I suppose you're going with some entirely fabricated story to Mrs. Cardew."

"If I should," Marcelle murmured, "I think Miss Shaw would 'ave to go."

Peter hesitated, all his natural loathing of underhand methods coming to the top. At the same time if he knew Marcelle she was more than capable of getting Beverley dismissed. He was interested in the children, and he disliked the idea of the first chance they had of becoming decent citizens being snatched from them. His experience with natives had taught him that there were times when for something worthwhile a little tipping had to be. He pulled out his notecase and shoved ten shillings into Marcelle's outstretched hand.

"Here you are. I wish I could have you for five minutes in an uncivilized country. I'd show you what we do with blackmailers."

Meggie, looking white-faced but herself, came into the children's sitting-room just before the walkers returned.

"How do you feel?" Beverley asked.

"All right. Sort of wobbly in the knees, and afraid I'll be cross very easily."

Beverley laughed.

"How well I know that feeling."

Meggie wandered round the room in a restless way.

"I wish it wasn't your half-Sunday. I like Annie, of course, but Mummy's going to be out all day with Peter, and there's nobody much to talk to."

Beverley had a sudden vision of Meggie still feeling nervous and on edge, shut up with Betsy being a panda, and David anything that made a noise. She looked forward to her half-days, but a rush of pity made her forget herself.

"How would you like to come out with me this afternoon?"

She was rewarded by the child's expression of pleasure, which was out of all proportion to the amusement offered.

"Oh, you wouldn't take me with you?"

"It won't be much fun. I meet a friend called Sarah. She's a governess, too. We have tea together somewhere."

"I'd love to come. Who's your friend governess to?"

"Some people called Elton. He's a parson, and terribly poor; Mrs. Elton's an invalid. I'll ring Sarah up and see whether she can bring the eldest girl with her. You and she are about the same age."

Betsy, enjoying her day as a panda, and David full of a scheme for staging the execution of Mary Queen of Scots with a doll whose head had come loose, saw Beverley and Meggie off with equanimity.

"I'm sorry you'll miss the execution," David said to Beverley. "There's a bit of old sponge soaked in red ink stuck in her neck, and when my axe drops, if I hit hard enough the blood will simply spurt."

Betsy turned up her nose.

"Thank goodness I'm a panda, and pandas aren't interested in hist'ry."

Meggie and Beverley walked across Piccadilly and into the Green Park. Mr. Elton's parish lay just over Westminster Bridge, so the meeting-place was the bridge over the water in St. James's Park. It was a lovely afternoon, cold, with a nip of frost in the air; the sun was shining and the sky was blue, and already the parks were glowing with flowers from the early bulbs. Meggie tucked her arm into Beverley's.

"I do feel better."

"Good, darling. You'll feel better still by the time we've had a real walk." She had known that this was her moment to talk to Meggie, but she was uncertain how to begin. "I was pleased you gave me those photographs and that letter."

Meggie flushed.

"I suppose you think it's awfully sloppy."

Beverley looked out over a group of small children playing soldiers.

"Not in themselves. There's no reason why you shouldn't have written to him about the play, or been given a photograph of him. But I think keeping the things under your mattress rather silly. I mean, why not have put the photograph in a frame if you wanted to have it about?"

Meggie scowled at the path.

"I didn't want Mummy teasing me."

"I don't suppose she would. Anyway, why should she notice it, she never comes to your room." Meggie raised her head.

"Everything sounds so easy to you. But in our house everybody talks. Betsy and Marcelle."

"Well, you give them cause to if you hide things under your mattress. Whoever makes your bed is bound to know they're there."

"Oh, no." Meggie looked shocked. "I keep them in a drawer until the room's done."

"But why all this secrecy? It makes a perfectly harmless friendship seem as though there was something wrong with it."

They were on the bridge now. Meggie hung over on the Buckingham Palace side.

"I wish the baby ducks were out."

Beverley was not to be put off by ducks.

"Why this secrecy?"

Meggie's mouth set in a stubborn line.

"I want a friend of my own. If Mummy saw the photograph I think she'd keep it."

"Meggie! Of course she wouldn't."

"Why not? Peter was our friend to start with. So was a man called Sir William Kent. We met him at grandmother's. Peter we found at a party; Mummy never noticed him till he came to see us. Then she sucked him in like everybody else. If you want a friend in our house, at least if it's a man friend, it's got to be a secret."

Beverley felt as if she were skating on ice in a thaw.

"But, my dear, why can't you share your friends with your mother? After all, you share Mr. Crewdson."

"We can't, because presently Mummy quarrels with them and won't let them come to the house. That was what happened to Sir William. He was awfully nice. We were simply miserable when he couldn't come any more. So this time I'm not taking any risk."

"When do you see him?"

Meggie sighed.

"Not often. He's an actor and he goes away. But at Christmas he took us to the circus, and he took me and Betsy to the ballet, and he said he'd take me to the National Gallery, but he went on tour first."

"You said you didn't like the National Gallery."

Meggie gave another sigh.

"Not with the others coming; anyway, I don't care much for pictures, but of course with the right person anything is nice."

Beverley laughed.

"Really, Meggie! I never heard such rubbish. You've been listening to crooners or something on the wireless."

Meggie gazed thoughtfully at Buckingham Palace.

"No." Her voice had a pathetic ring. "I didn't think you'd understand exactly. You aren't that kind of person. But you see, I haven't many friends, so I treasure those I have. Once I had Nanny and Sir William, and George.

Now out of those there's only George. There's you as a new one." Her voice tailed away, "But how do I know you won't go?"

Beverley wondered. How indeed? It was obvious in a house like number ten anybody could go at a moment's notice if Mrs. Cardew felt like it.

"You've forgotten Mr. Crewdson," she said lightly.

Meggie's incredible Mediterranean blue eyes looked into hers. Beverley was shocked at the disillusionment in them.

"Sez you!" Then she added: "As man to man would you call him our friend now?"

"Yes." Beverley repeated the word more firmly. "*Yes.* You can't expect him to spend all his time in the nursery, but I think he's a wonderful friend to you children."

The look of disillusionment in Meggie's eyes deepened.

"We'll be lucky if he's not a relation."

To Beverley's relief Sarah arrived with the eldest Elton. She was a long-legged, plain child called Miriam. Beside the exquisitely dressed Meggie she looked pitiably shabby. The two girls were sent on to walk together. Beverley looked in dismay at their backs.

"Isn't it awful? I've hardly been living amongst money any time, and already it's blunted me. Do you know I've begun not to notice how awfully grandly my children are dressed."

Sarah sighed.

"I can never forget how badly mine are. Half my life is spent patching, and the other half letting out and letting down. Now come on, tell me about the matinée."

Meggie and Miriam took to each other at sight. Their worlds were so wildly unalike that hearing of each other's daily doings was like seeing a film. To Miriam, Meggie's knowledge of theatres and theatre people was awe-inspiring and a little shocking, and Meggie couldn't tell her enough about it. But equally Meggie found Miriam's world amazing.

"Tell me about things in your house."

"Well, Mummy's ill, you know, and Coxy," she nodded at Sarah, "does all the looking after us, and quite a lot of the cooking, too. Of course I help."

Meggie blinked.

"Why do you?"

"Well, somebody's got to. We've only one maid, and she's mostly answering the front door. Doors at vicarages ring an awful lot."

"Do they?"

"Oh, yes," Miriam sighed. "We take turns taking up Mummy's trays. Hannah can't take one yet, she's only six, but Marjorie and I do. Then we sit with Mummy while she eats."

"Doesn't she have lots of people to see her?"

"Sometimes. Parish workers and people like that, but she likes it best when there's nobody but us. I think mothers are like that."

Meggie flushed and changed the subject.

The four of them had tea at the Strand Corner House. It was a cheerful meal. Beverley was amazed at the improvement in Meggie. Almost before they had sat down she was tugging at her sleeve.

"Miss Shaw, Miss Cox takes the Eltons to places on Saturdays, too. Couldn't we meet?"

"Couldn't we, Coxy?" Miriam put in.

Sarah looked at Beverley.

"I don't see why not. I must ask Mrs. Elton, of course, but I'm sure she'd like it. Do you think Mrs. Cardew would mind?"

Meggie looked anxiously at Beverley, who gave her a reassuring smile.

"I'm sure she won't. Remind me to ask Miss Winks tomorrow, Meggie."

Meggie's eyes shone.

"I know what, we'll telephone. The Eltons shall choose one week, and the Cardews the other."

Miriam looked doubtful.

"We don't use the telephone much. It's for Daddy for the parish; it costs a lot."

Beverley smiled at her.

"Meggie shall ring you. She loves telephoning."

"There's another thing," said Sarah. "Most of the places will have to be free. We haven't many pennies."

Meggie nodded.

"I'd thought of that. We must go to free places, and, if they're a long way off it must be on a day when we have the car. Mummy said the other day she would get a car and a chauffeur for the schoolroom, but she hasn't yet, so we have to share with her." Sarah glanced at Miriam, and they all laughed. To Beverley's delight it was Meggie who said, "It does sound silly, doesn't it?"

On the way home Meggie caught hold of and hugged

Beverley's arm.

"Thank you so much," she hesitated and then added awkwardly, "I suppose we couldn't call you something else than Miss Shaw, could we? You know, like Coxy."

Beverley laughed.

" 'Shawy' sounds a bit odd."

Meggie nodded.

"It does, but there must be something. I'll ask the others. You wouldn't mind, would you?"

"Mind! Of course not. I'd like it."

The rest of Sunday being their own, Beverley and Sarah deposited their charges and rejoined each other in Soho for dinner. Talking over their work, the time passed like lightning and it was nearly eleven when Beverley put her latchkey into the lock at number ten. The hall was in semi-darkness, but the drawing-room door was open, and through it light streamed and Margot's voice rang out.

"Do stop making conversation." Her voice dropped. "Do you love me at all, Peter?"

Peter did not answer immediately. When he did his words came with the slowness of someone fumbling for the exact truth.

"I admire you enormously and—"

There was the sound of a smack.

"Shut up. I don't want any damned artificial politeness. I'm in love and I asked you a question."

His voice took on the soothing note he would use on a frightened horse.

"Don't get all worked up. You didn't give me time to finish. The truth is, Margot, you're blinding like the

125

sunlight. I can't see clearly when I'm looking at you."

"Oh, blast you." Margot was obviously crying. "You're always wanting to be sure of things. Can't you take anything for granted?"

"Not love."

"Is there somebody else?"

"No. You know you're tired or you wouldn't be talking like this."

"It's not tiredness—I know you think it's queer that I ask you to marry me. But why not? I'm not like other women. I see what I want and I don't hang around pining for it. I go and get it. Well, I want you. Why not? You may not be utterly in love with me now, but you will be. Besides, I could be useful to you. I know—"

His voice was firm.

"When I marry I shan't marry because my wife can be useful to me. I shall marry because I'm desperately in love."

"Are you so sure you're not?"

"I'm fascinated and under your spell, but that isn't love, at least not my kind."

Evidently he showed signs of going, for Margot's voice came urgently:

"Don't go."

"I must. It's late."

"You'll come back. You won't let what I've said put you off—stop you coming to the house?"

"My dear, I must. It will be a good thing—it might make me see clearly."

"No, no, no. Forget all I've said. Let's just be friends."

He was laughing.

"What a woman you are. Any intimate conversation with you is played like the big emotional scene in the third act."

Beverley had not known what to do. Scarlet to the ears, she had stood still in the middle of the hall wondering whether to cough and let them know she was there, or to run up the stairs. The running won because she felt it would be so awful for Margot to realize she had been overheard. But however hard you try, it's impossible to run quietly in the dark. But at the third step of the stairs she stumbled. Fortunately Margot was too intent on what she was saying to hear. Unwillingly Beverley had to creep, and as she crept every word from the drawing-room reached her. She tried whispering to cut out the sounds. "Peter Piper picked a peck of pickled pepper—" But it was no good. No Peter Piper could cut out what those two in the drawing-room were saying. "Never mind. After the first landing I can run," she thought.

As she reached the landing Margot and Peter came into the hall. Beverley did not look, but the sounds came plainly.

"Kiss me good night." There was a pause. "God, you'd kiss your grandmother like that."

Beverley was on the landing. In one second her foot would be on the next flight. Then something made her glance along the corridor. The dim light from the hall showed a figure leaning over the balustrade; it was Marcelle.

Horrified, Beverley raced to her room. She sat on her

bed feeling sick. "How could she?" she whispered. "How could she? A great actress like that to make herself so cheap. And Marcelle sneaking and prying." She clasped her hands. "In a house like this, how can I bring up those children to be nice? How can I?" She got up and began taking off her things. Suddenly she stopped, her frock in one hand. "I'm glad he doesn't love her. Oh, I am glad."

CHAPTER EIGHT

BEVERLEY walked across the park. The sun was shining; it was Thursday, but her heart was in her boots. Suddenly she heard a "hullo". Looking up, she saw Peter sitting on a chair under a tree.

"Hullo."

He got up.

"Where are you off to?"

"Thursday is my half-day. I'm going to meet a friend presently; she's at the dentist."

He smiled.

"As you came along you looked as if you were going to the dentist. I never saw anything so depressed."

Beverley nodded.

"I was, and I am. Life's being just awful in our house."

"Is it? I haven't been there this week." Beverley would have liked to say, "That's partly the trouble." He nodded at his chair and one beside it. "Why don't we sit?" He waited until she was settled. "Come on, let's swop troubles."

She looked up at him sympathetically.

"Have you some, too?"

"What do you think?"

Beverley was not quite sure what to answer. Privately she thought it a very good thing he was not seeing so much of Margot; but, of course, he was probably missing her very badly.

"I suppose you have."

"You bet. You know I loathe being idle. Sometimes when I wake up in the morning with nothing to do all day, except eat and drink in somebody's house or have someone coming to eat and drink with me, I think I'll go mad."

Beverley screwed up her face.

"I'm awfully sorry for you, but you know I think it's your own fault. If I'd been ill and wasn't allowed to work, the last place I'd be in would be London."

He gave her an amused look.

"What a girl you are for jumping to conclusions. Did you think I was hanging about London from choice?"

"Yes."

"Well, you're wrong. If I had my way I'd spend the time fishing. Fishing's a grand sport, you know."

"Well, why don't you?"

"Because I'm having treatment; three days a week I have a shot of bugs put in me."

Beverley gave herself a mental shake. What a habit she had, as he said, of jumping to conclusions. Much as she liked him, she had always vaguely scorned the way he hung about, apparently at a permanent loose end. He looked down at her.

"Come on, it's your turn. What's your particular grouse?"

"This charity matinée. You never knew such a fuss. It's made the children difficult just as they were being really nice."

"What are they doing at the show?"

"Nothing. Just standing about being pottery. But Mrs. Cardew has been rehearsing the last three nights, and she doesn't know her words and the children fidget and then there's trouble. Oh, it's all nothing really. I expect I've got a liver."

"You don't look a bit like it."

She fidgeted with the fingers of her gloves.

"Then I do hate Marcelle."

He gave her a quick look.

"What's she been saying to you?"

"Nothing. But she looks knowing, as if she and I shared a secret, and I wouldn't share anything with her. I don't trust her and I feel mean about her. I saw her once listening to something that was nothing to do with her, and I think I ought to have had the courage to go and tell her what I thought of her."

"Any further troubles?"

She longed to say, "Yes, ever since Sunday I've carried yours and Margot's secret in my head, and I hate it. I'm not that sort of a person." Instead she got up.

"I'd better have a brisk walk. It's what I need."

He got up too.

"Can I go with you?"

She laughed.

"It sounds as if I ought to answer, 'Yes, if you please, kind sir.' But as a matter of fact I'm going to say 'no'. I've got a black dog on my shoulder and I'll get rid of it better alone."

"Sure? I've had a lot of troubles with black dogs of my own. I'm getting quite good at shaking them off."

She suddenly nodded.

"Come on, then." They walked towards Buckingham Palace.

"How's Meggie?" he asked.

"She's nervous. She's at the awkward age, and rehearsing with her mother scares her stiff. You know Mrs. Cardew can't move any way but beautifully and she doesn't understand other people who can't." She made her voice casual. "They're all missing you."

To her surprise he answered quite seriously:

"I feel I've let them down. You've no right to make friends with kids, and make a habit of calling in to see them, and then suddenly drop them. But as a matter of fact I've had things to do lately."

He finished so lamely that Beverley, sympathizing with his need for an excuse, broke in:

"Well, just send them a message, or a letter."

He shoved his hands in his pockets.

"There's no need for that. As a matter of fact I had a telephone call from Mrs. Cardew this morning. I said I'd look in tomorrow."

Beverley kept her face away from him. How she wished she had not been forced to hear that scene on Sunday night. It made it so awkward; here he was talking casually of a telephone call, and here was she picturing Margot's frenzied calls and promises, and his final capitulation.

He left her on the bridge in St. James's Park, where she was meeting Sarah, but after he had gone few steps he came back.

"Would you come and dine with me one Thursday?"

Her breath was taken away, the invitation was so unexpected.

"I'd love to."

"Next Thursday?"

"Yes."

He smiled.

"That'll be something to look forward to."

She grinned.

"I don't see why. Just somebody else eating and drinking with you."

He nodded.

"I deserved that, and I'm not going to make the obvious retort that you aren't just somebody else. Shall we say the Apèritif at eight o'clock, and we won't dress."

Beverley watched him go, and was still watching when Sarah arrived.

"Good gracious," said Sarah. "What's happened? Somebody left you a fortune?"

Beverley flushed.

"Hullo. No. Why?"

Sarah opened her bag and took out her mirror.

"Have a look at your face."

Beverley glanced in the glass and saw the sparkle in her eyes. She pushed the glass away.

"If you want to know, I've been asked out to dinner by Mr. Crewdson. I met him in the park. It's not very exciting really, only going out to dinner is fun."

Sarah raised her left eyebrow.

"Didn't you tell me he was Mrs. Cardew's number one man?"

"Yes, but she's in the theatre at dinner-time, and he's been ill. He just wants company."

Sarah gave her a shrewd look.

"Why I ever got fond of you, Beverley Shaw, I don't know. For as sure as eggs are eggs I'll be digging you out of a mess before I'm through."

During breakfast the next morning, Winkle rang through on the house phone.

"Is that you, dear? It's about the dress rehearsal this afternoon. Could you slip down for a moment so we get everything clear?"

Winkle was fond of asking Beverley to slip down. She was always wanting to get something clear and only believed it could be made clear in her study. To Beverley, slipping down was difficult. Every second of her morning was planned and getting away for five minutes needed scheming.

"Is that about that awful dress rehearsal?" asked Meggie.

Beverley nodded.

Betsy sighed and helped herself to toast.

"It's all right for you, Meggie. You can lean against the cow."

Meggie savagely cut her bread in half.

"It's that elbow. I can't get it right. I never milked a cow, so of course I look awkward. Then the prologue's so long—if I do get in the right position I get pins and needles and you can't sit still with them."

David took a drink of milk.

"You don't know what trouble is, Meggie, until you're me and have to kiss Betsy all the time."

Betsy spread her toast with honey.

"I like that; I have to have your mouth on my cheek. It's just as bad for me."

Beverley poured herself out a second cup of coffee.

"You're making a lot of fuss. The whole thing doesn't take five minutes. You can all stay still that long."

"Are you coming with us?" Meggie asked.

Beverley nodded.

"I believe so."

"You will go in front and tell us how we look, won't you?" Betsy urged.

"I'd much rather you were in the wings," said Meggie.

David sighed.

"I wish I could drink glue or something so I'd know no bit of me would jerk."

Beverley laughed.

"Poor old man. I tell you what—don't think about keeping still. Just before you go on the stage I'll give you a subject and each of you make up a rhyme about it, and the one of you who thinks of the best shall have a prize."

"What prize?" asked Betsy.

Beverley sipped her coffee.

"Anything within reason. If you win you can choose what you wear when you go out with the Eltons on Saturday."

"If I win," said David, " I shall miss drill."

"And if I win"—Meggie took a piece of bread—"I shall go out with you again on Sunday."

"If I were you, Shawskins," said Betsy, "I'd see she didn't win. You don't want to have to take *her,* do you?"

135

Beverley smiled.

"The judging will be fair, but if anybody fidgets they don't win, however good their rhyme is."

After breakfast Beverley went down to Winkle.

"Oh, there you are, dear." Winkle blinked at her anxiously through her glasses. "Now let me see, where is that slip?" She rummaged amongst her papers. "Oh, yes, the car will be here at three-thirty to take you, the children and their dresses, and Annie, to the theatre. Mrs. Cardew is speaking her prologue at the end of the rehearsal instead of the beginning because she has her rest in the afternoon."

"Three-thirty," Beverley repeated. "We'll be ready."

"Thank you, dear." Winkle pushed her glasses down her nose. "You've no idea what a comfort to me it is having you. Nanny was a dear, but at the end she argued about any order and it did make things so difficult."

Beverley laughed.

"I bet it did." She gave Winkle a sympathetic glance. "You look tired."

Winkle's eyes dimmed with tears.

"It's been a terrible week. You know, Mr. Crewdson hasn't been near us, and he does have such a soothing effect."

Beverley looked pityingly at Winkle, though inwardly wondering if "soothing" was the word she would have used if she had overheard Margot on Sunday night.

"You shouldn't let her upset you."

Winkle snatched her handkerchief out of her pocket and rubbed her eyes and glasses.

"You are quite right. Very silly of me, and anyway, Mr. Crewdson is coming today. But it hasn't been only him. Mrs. Cardew has begun to study her part in the new play; the 'Last weeks' notice is out about the present one, you know."

"No, I didn't."

"Oh, yes, and I do wish she'd found another nice woman to act. You've no idea how pleasant she was when she was rehearsing Sybil in the present play. You've seen it, so you remember how Sybil grows nicer and nicer as the play goes on. Well, so did Mrs. Cardew when she was studying. She was so considerate that often I wondered if she were ill. But now she's working at this new play *Helen* she quite frightens me sometimes."

"Why?"

"Well, of course, it's only acting, we all know that, but she is a murderess, you know, murdering for jealousy. Just, sometimes when she's studying, she gets a look on her face which almost makes me cry out." She glanced from Beverley to the open window. "Is that too much; you shivered?"

Beverley shook her head.

"No. A goose walked over my grave."

"My," said Annie, "a nice job these'll be to get into the theatre without crushing."

Beverley looked at the children's three glazed chintz costumes.

"Won't they fold?"

"Fold!" Annie sniffed. "They're mounted on stiffened

137

buckram. They'd crack if you bent them."

David swung on the end of the banister.

"And they scratch awf'ly."

Betsy, very cheerful in her ermine coat, hopped round the hall.

"All the little flowers on mine are painted by hand, and the dressmaker said I looked a perfect picture, didn't she, Annie?"

Annie sniffed again.

"If she'd known you as well as I do, it's a funny kind of picture she'd have called you."

Winkle, more like the white rabbit than usual, fussed down the stairs.

"Have you everything? The clothes, the shoes and stockings, and the tea-basket?"

Meggie looked at her in reproach.

"Shawskins never forgets anything."

"Oh, I know, dear," Winkle peered through the glass of the hall door, "but one can't help being anxious. Your mother will be so upset if anything goes wrong. Oh dear, dear, the car is late."

Beverley looked at her watch.

"No, I set this by T.I.M. this morning; it isn't quite half-past."

"That was very sensible of you, dear. Ah, there it is. Now in you all get. Annie, you better go in front with the dresses."

Annie looked scornful.

"What, with these!"

Winkle looked more flustered than ever, so Beverley

138

took command.

"Betsy and Meggie will go in front. Now, Betsy, no arguing. No, it can't be David, he's coming inside with me. In you get, Annie, and take all the room you want. I can take David on my knee."

The matinée was not being performed at Margot's theatre, but at another. A dressing-room had been allotted to the children, but it was, of course, only lent for the afternoon, and the make-up and clothes of the two actresses whose room it was were just covered with chintz.

"My," said Annie gloomily, as she hung up the children's dresses, "let's hope we aren't kept waiting long or this room will look as though a donkey'd been loose in it."

Beverley, leaving the children with Annie, went along to find Margot's dressing-room. She was not used to backs of stages and felt shy as she pressed herself against the walls to let first eight girls appearing in a ballet, and then a man dressed as a Hamlet, and a woman as Ophelia, go by. She was even more embarrassed when she found the stairs leading to Margot's room crammed with people dressed as Greeks. They made room for her to pass, but carried straight on with what they were saying as if she were not there.

"My dear, *have* you seen Elsbeth? Titania! I nearly said to her, 'You look divine as queen of the elephants.' "

A young man in a very brief bit of drapery took a deep breath so that Beverley could wriggle by, and talked to another young man over her head.

"I said to him it may be a good part, old man, but I've had co-billing with Lucia Lay in *Greenaway Blues* and I won't be put off with miserable-size type while that Sydney Sale girl is starred in great black letters. Well, I think that's right, don't you? After all, who is Sydney Sale, anyway?"

Mrs. Brown, as Beverley had hoped, was in Margot's room. She looked up with a puzzled frown, as Beverley's head came round the door. Then her face cleared.

"Oh, you're the children's governess. Stupid of me to go forgetting. Come in, dear. You got the children here?"

"Yes, it's about them. I was wondering if there's any way of you letting me know when Mrs. Cardew arrives. The children can't sit once they're dressed, and, of course, they mustn't be late."

Mrs. Brown nodded.

"Tell the door-keeper to send down. Even in these charity shows the door-keeper generally keeps his head."

Beverley felt at home with Mrs. Brown.

"I'm not used to theatres. Is it all right for me to give the door-keeper an order?"

Mrs. Brown laughed.

"No harm in a little"— She closed her right hand and rubbed the fingers over the palm. "Sixpence would do." She saw Beverley's doubtful face. "You come along with me. We've worked here; I know him."

Back in the dressing-room, secure in the doorkeeper's promise to call them directly Margot arrived, Beverley told Annie to unpack the tea-basket. Though she made it linger out as long as possible, she could not make pretence

140

that tea was not finished by half-past four, and by that time Betsy and David were out of hand.

"Why can't we go in the passage, Shawskins?" Betsy grumbled. "We always have."

David climbed up on to one of the dressing-tables.

"Let's play who can get round the room without touching the ground."

Beverley pulled David back to the floor and opened her bag and took out a pack of cards.

"We'll play 'Happy Families'. Come, Annie, you play, too. We'll all sit on the floor."

It was a tiresome sort of game; neither Betsy nor David really had their minds on it, and nothing but Beverley's imperturbable good humour and firmness kept them at it. It was a relief to them all when, at five o'clock, the doorkeeper knocked on the door.

"Miss Dale is in, Miss."

From the moment that they knew Margot had arrived they all felt they had to bustle. Beverley did keep her head, and kept saying, "It's all right, Annie, there's plenty of time." "Don't fidget, David. How can Annie button your smock if you hop about?" "All right, Betsy, give me the comb. I'll do your hair, though there's plenty of time."

When dressed, Beverley felt proud of the children. The dresses were really charming in neo-Watteau style. They were glazed white chintz, but the flowers on Meggie's hat and the bunches of flowers on her frock were cherry coloured. Betsy had sky-blue flowers on hers, and a little bunch of blue bows on the end of a white crook. David's smock and breeches were white, but at his knees were tags of olive-green ribbon.

"Can we go down to Mummy now?" asked David.

It was plain that all three children were nervous. Beverley, knowing they could not sit in the dresses, thought it was a mistake to keep them hanging about.

"I'll go and see your mother, if you promise to stay where you are till I come back."

Once more Beverley pushed her way down the passages. They seemed more crowded than ever. Evidently the matinée was finishing with some sort of empire effect, for she met Canada and attendants, and New Zealand and attendants, and a Rajah, and ten girls dressed as Irish colleens, but this time there was nobody standing gossiping outside Margot's door. Beverley gave an inward smile.

"I bet they haven't the nerve," she thought. "I can hear what she'd say."

Mrs. Brown opened the door in answer to her knock.

"Yes, dear?" she asked, and as she spoke she gave a slow, meaning wink with her left eye.

Beverley did not know what the wink meant.

"Would you ask Mrs. Cardew if the children may come down and show her their dresses?"

"Oh, is that Miss Shaw?" Margot's voice was fretful. "No, I can't have them now. I'll see them on the stage. Take them down to the side of the stage. Tell the stage manager I said they were to watch the show until I'm ready. And, Mrs. Brown, go down and see if the cow is here, and has got a wreath round its neck. I can't think why Winkle isn't here. I ought not to have to see to everything myself, it's ridiculous."

Mrs. Brown closed the door and came into the passage, but not before Beverley had noticed a chuckle. To her surprise her heart seemed to miss a beat.

"That's Mr. Crewdson, isn't it?"

"That's right." Mrs. Brown hurried along the passage. "I'm glad to see him, too. Been playing up shocking she has. Not that he's helping much. Very offhand. Making her wild, he is." She stopped before an iron door marked "Stage. Silence please." "Course nobody's asking me but I think she's barking up the wrong tree. No matter who you are it's no good saying snip if Mr. Right won't say snap."

Beverley was unconscious that she hurried back to the children with shining eyes. She did not know why she was so glad. She would have denied it if anybody had told her that her heart sang a Te Deum because it was no good Margot saying snip unless Peter said snap.

Nothing could have been more unpopular than the arrival of the Cardew children on the side of the stage. A sketch was in progress, which required absolute silence. The stage manager tip-toed towards Beverley scowling.

"Take those children back to their dressing-room."

The stage manager meant nothing in Beverley's life, and Margot a lot. She answered in a calm whisper.

"They're Miss Dale's children and she says they're to be here."

He ran a hand through his hair.

"But the tableau's next. A hundred and sixty on at once. Where do you think I'm going to put these children?"

Beverley grinned.

"I don't have to think. If you say they can't stop I'll go to Miss Dale and tell her so."

He caught her arm.

"For God's sake don't. All right, take them in the O.P. and for heaven's sake keep them quiet."

He scuttled off and Beverley went back to the children.

"What's the O.P.?"

"Opposite prompt. Down there." Meggie pointed down stage right.

The sketch was dull and the two stars acting it hardly knew a word.

"My goodness," Betsy hissed at Meggie. "Can you see Mummy giving a performance like that?"

Beverley frowned.

"Ssh."

"But they are awful," said David.

"Ssh." Beverley whispered again.

"I don't see why we need ssh," Betsy argued. "They can't hear anything but the prompter."

Beverley remembered how impressed she had been at their behaviour at their mother's matinée. She tried now appealing to their pride.

She pulled Betsy and David out of the wings.

"I should have thought you two would know how to behave in a theatre."

Betsy flushed.

"We do. Only they're so bad."

Fortunately at that moment the curtain fell, and at once Meggie gave Beverley's arm a pull.

"Come on."

144

To Beverley's surprise she found herself on the stage with her back to the tabs. She looked nervously at the stage manager, supposing they would get turned off, but evidently the children knew what was right. The scenery was being changed and they were in the one place where they could not be in the way.

Thrilled as anybody must be who is unused to a theatre, she watched the wings fly up into the roof and the cottage front disappear and the whole stage hung in purple curtains. She watched rostrums built up and covered in purple cloth and a flight of steps put in place. Meanwhile all the actors who were to appear were streaming on to the stage.

The stage manager looked round.

"Are the angels here yet?" A group of girls in white with little halos and large wings stepped forward. He pointed to some canvas clouds being lowered from the flies. "There's your clouds, girls."

The clouds caused some delay. Each cloud was to take two girls, lying or standing in ecstatic but awkward positions. None of the girls liked the look of the clouds.

"I won't get up till the last minute."

"And don't forget when we are up, that we're there. If you want to take it through twice let the clouds down."

"Oh, come on, girls. They're quite safe," the stage manager urged.

"They may be, but they don't look it. You put up your dominions and we'll get up afterwards."

With a lot of fussing the dominions were arranged. Britannia the centrepiece was an opera singer and gave an immense amount of trouble. She couldn't see the conductor's baton, her attendants hid her train, Canada and Africa were standing too close; and the more she complained the more all the assembled actresses and actors muttered behind their hands. At last, however, they were all settled, and the unwilling angels hoisted into place.

"Clear," said the stage manager. The children and Beverley scurried back into the wings. "Lights." The stage was bathed in amber, Britannia standing out in a spotlight, the angels flooded in a pink glow. The stage manager pressed a button. The conductor raised his baton, the curtain rose, and at that moment Margot, exquisite in glazed chintz, forced her way through the actors on to the stage.

"Oh, one moment. I'm sure none of you would mind, would you, if I said my prologue first?" She turned smiling to the cast. "It won't take a moment."

"But—but—Miss Dale—" the stage manager bleated. "We shan't be long over this either, and I've just got it set. I've got black velvet curtains to lower for you."

"Now, don't fuss," Margot smiled graciously. "I'll manage without my curtains. Where are the children? Where's my cow?"

The children, even Betsy, turned horrified faces up to Beverley.

"Oh, Mummy can't do it now. They're all set," Meggie whispered. "Everybody is simply hating her, I can feel it. Oh, please, Shawskins, do ask her to wait."

Betsy unexpectedly crouched against Beverley like a

146

scared chicken under its mother.

"Oh, dear, Mummy's going to have one of her scenes."

David's face was scarlet.

"Oh, I wish we needn't do it."

Beverley leant down and put an arm round Betsy, and took David's hand.

"Don't fuss, darlings. We'll all be back home laughing in half an hour. Now you think of the verse you're going to make up. I want it about jam."

The opera singer had held up her hand. The children watched her with horrified eyes.

"This is past making up rhymes," Meggie whispered. "There's going to be an awful row."

"What is this delay?" demanded the opera singer.

"Where are the children?" said Margot.

"Go on, darlings." Beverley gave them a slight push. She felt a beast to do it, they looked so small and shrinking. "And don't forget 'Jam.' "

The stage manager was whispering imploringly to the opera singer.

"Ah, there you are," Margot called to the children. "Let me see your frock-ums. Turn round, Betsy. Oh, 'oo has got a pritsum crook. Now let me see you, Meggie. Very pretty frock, but not a very pretty face. These little china figures smile. Oh, look at my boykins, isn't 'oo a pet."

The reactions of the cast on the stage could have been felt by someone blind, deaf and dumb. The children, bitterly ashamed, hunched up their shoulders, scowled, and stood in a tight, embarrassed group.

"Now where is the cow?" asked Margot.

147

The stage manager, who had just succeeded in placating the opera singer, bustled down stage.

"It's coming. Props. Miss Dale's cow."

"Coming, sir," said a voice off. Wheels were heard, and presently a life size black and white cow, garlanded with mixed flowers, was pushed on to the stage.

"Isn't it a sweetums," said Margot. She turned to the men. "And the milking stools?" Three white stools were produced. "That's right. Now, children, positions."

At all times the positions were trying ones. Meggie had to milk the cow; Betsy to sit on a stool looking coy while David on another beside her kissed her cheek. Today, conscious of a hundred and sixty pairs of angry eyes on their necks, let alone the angry eyes of the stage hands in the wings and the flies, they became muscle bound. Even Betsy, to whom posing came as natural as walking, sat awkwardly with a painful smirk on her face. Margot gave one look at them, and all the colour faded under her make-up. She tapped her foot on the stage, her hands shook.

"Children! What are you doing? Do you want to disgrace poor Mummy? Take your positions properly at once."

Beverley clasped her hands.

"I shouldn't look," a voice whispered behind her. "You can't do anything."

Beverley felt a sudden quite unreasoned relief. It seemed to her that Peter's mere presence was a help. She gave him a rueful glance.

"I quite see a person as clever as Mrs. Cardew doesn't

grasp it, but this sort of thing is torture to these children."

He nodded.

"Don't I know."

"My dear Meggie, look at that elbow," came Margot's voice. "And David, that isn't how Mummy told you to hold your head. Not that dreadful grin, Betsy, a pretty little smile."

"I say," came a voice from one of the clouds, "if this is going on much longer, you might let these clouds down. I'm getting cramp in my stomach."

"And I'm sure they're not safe," said another angel.

"And if they are safe," a third grumbled, "the motion is awful. They sway all the time. I never was a good sailor. Look pretty if the angels are sick."

Margot, obviously controlling her temper, gazed up at the clouds.

"My dear young ladies, when you've been on the stage a few more years you will learn that there are worse discomforts than lying on clouds attached to your art. However, I'll begin now. I'll take these children through their positions at home."

"Lights," said the stage manager thankfully. The stage darkened and a steel-blue glow was thrown on Margot and the children. "Drop the curtain." The tabs swung together. He pressed another button and they swung up again.

Margot gave the pause necessary for the tableau to be taken in. Then she broke from her pose and held out her arms.

" 'Oh, England, on whose soil strange, lovely sights

have passed—' "

There was an ominous creak from the clouds.

" 'Renew our courage, and unbind our eyes—' "

There was a further creak. It was too much for David; he turned his head. Margot, none too sure of her words, lost their flow. She turned savagely on Betsy.

"How dare you move?"

"I didn't," said Betsy. "It was David."

"I had to," David wailed. "I did think the angels were going to fall."

"Be quiet," thundered Margot.

But Betsy, thoroughly shaken, lost her head and began to howl.

Margot shook her.

"Be quiet."

"I won't be quiet," sobbed Betty. "I want Shawskins. Where's Shawskins?"

Meggie looked desperately into the wings.

"Do come, Shawskins."

Without thinking of herself, Beverley came. She went straight into the glow of blue limelight and knelt by the children.

"Be quiet, Betsy. Let your mother finish." She gave her a dig in the ribs. "Cheer up, it'll soon be over." She held David's hands. "You'll only make things worse for the angels if you look round. It'll keep them longer." She gave Meggie's hand a squeeze, then turned to Margot. "I think it will be all right if you go on now." She went back into the wings.

Margot took a deep breath, all the rage in her heart on

the tip of her tongue. The stage manager saw what was coming.

"All right, Miss Dale. I'll lower the curtain, so you can start again."

Once more the curtain rose on the blue group. Once more Margot raised her arms.

" 'Oh, England, on whose soil strange, lovely sights have passed—' "

"And one of the lovely sights that will pass will be that governess," Mrs. Brown whispered to a stage hand, "or I don't know what's what."

The children, shaken and scared, hardly waited for the curtain to drop before they scurried after Beverley to their dressing-room.

"Well, how'd you do?" asked Annie.

Beverley, who was undoing Meggie's frock, made a face over her shoulder.

"It was all a bit of a muddle—dress rehearsals are, you know—but they looked lovely and I never heard anything more beautiful than the way Mrs. Cardew said the prologue."

Meggie glanced round gratefully.

"She did say it beautifully. Even if they hated being kept waiting, all those people must have thought that, mustn't they?"

There was a knock on the door and Mrs. Brown looked in.

"Mrs. Cardew wants to see you, Miss Shaw."

Betsy gave a scream and flung herself at Beverley.

"Don't go. She's going to send you away."

151

Beverley calmly pulled the child off her.

"Don't be so silly. It's only about the arrangements for the car going home."

Meggie had turned terribly white.

"You don't know. Suppose it isn't." Two huge tears rolled slowly down her cheeks. "You can't leave us. You can't."

David was sitting on the floor taking off his shoes. He looked up, his eyes rounded with fright.

"Go!" he said, and then added with a pitiable wobble, "You won't go away, will you, Shawskins?"

Beverley managed a laugh which she felt very unlike making.

"You are all very silly. I'll be back in five minutes. If you hurry, we'll just have time for a game when we get home before David goes to bed."

As the door shut on Beverley the children looked at each other.

"She doesn't know Mummy," Betsy whispered.

David dragged off his second shoe.

"I thought you didn't like her."

Betsy's voice was puzzled.

"I didn't know I did. I mean, not properly until today."

Annie glanced at Meggie and put her arm round her.

"Don't look like that, my pretty. You don't know she's going. It might just be about the car, as she says."

Betsy shook her head.

"It's not, Annie. You don't know what happened. It was simply awful. It was David's fault."

"Not altogether me, it wasn't. It was you that cried. I

152

only looked round." David turned to Annie. "There was angels on a cloud and the cloud made a noise when Mummy was acting, and then I had to turn round because I thought one of the angels was being sick, and I never saw an angel being sick."

Meggie, shivering, leant against Annie. Annie was shocked at her colour.

"Come on, Miss Meggie dear, you sit down and let me change your shoes and stockings."

Outside in the passage Mrs. Brown gave Beverley an expressive nod.

"She's in a nice taking. Won't let Mr. Crewdson or me say a word. Storming up and down the room, she is. 'Send me that girl,' she says. 'Where's that Miss Shaw? How dare she interfere between me and my children? And in front of everybody, too!' "

"Oh, well," said Beverley, more bravely than she felt, "I'd better get along, I suppose, and see what she wants."

"I can tell you what she wants. It's to give you the order of the boot." At Margot's dressing-room door Mrs. Brown stopped. "You go in alone, dear. I've seen her quarrel with so many good people in my time, I've no stomach for seeing her do it again."

Because her courage needed bolstering, Beverley unconsciously threw up her chin and straightened her shoulders before she faced Margot. Peter, leaning against the wall, felt his pulses stir as he looked at her. Once, some years before, he had seen a war to the death between a mongoose and a snake. It was a very small mongoose and a very powerful cobra. The result was

153

certain before the fight began, but the mongoose showed no sign of that, though doubtless he knew it. He gave a shake to his funny, long body and his little weasel legs, raised his pointed muzzle and went into the battle like a champion. And so did Beverley. Colour flamed in her cheeks; she had no hat on, and her red hair seemed to glitter, and there was a very valiant look in her grey-green eyes. Just for one second he and she exchanged a look. His said, "I'm here if I can be any help." Hers said, "It's nice having you there, but I'm perfectly capable of fighting my own battles, thank you."

Margot had still got on her stage things and makeup. When the door opened she was walking up and down the room, but as Beverley came in she stopped and faced her. Her whole body was shaking; only by gripping her hands together could she keep them still.

"Miss Shaw, how dared you behave as you did this afternoon?"

Beverley opened her eyes.

"In what way?"

"Coming on to the stage. Insulting me before practically the whole of the theatrical profession. Giving the impression that my children obeyed you rather than me."

"I never looked at it like that. You had all the prologue to remember. I just thought that since you were paying me to look after them, the least I could do was to see they were quiet."

"Since when have they called you by that ridiculous nickname?"

"It is silly—they've only taken to it the last day or two.

You know how children like nicknames."

"I don't. In any case, it's a small point, for they will not have a chance to call you that or anything else in future. You are dismissed. You can leave tomorrow. Winkle will pay you whatever is due to you."

The colour deepened in Beverley's cheeks.

"Very well," she agreed quietly. "But as I'm going I'd just like to tell you something. It wasn't me who disgraced you before the theatrical profession this afternoon. It was you who disgraced yourself in front of your children."

"What! How dare you!"

Beverley swept on, disregarding Margot's anger.

"If you could have seen what happened you'd have been ashamed. I don't believe you have any idea how proud those children are of you. Even David positively bursts with pride when you come on the stage. This afternoon they saw the trouble the stage manager had to get that tableau ready, and they saw the effect you had when you interrupted it. If you could have seen your children's shocked faces you would never have done it. They are grand children; when I've gone, don't forget how proud they are of you, and how you hurt them when you let them down."

Her real emotion and indignation had brought a lump into her throat. She did not want Margot to know, so she turned to the door.

Margot held up a finger.

"No, don't go." She seemed stunned, and felt for her words. "Are they really so proud of me?"

Beverley swallowed the lump. Her eyes were shining

155

with unshed tears.

"What do you think? Wouldn't you be proud of a mother who was as splendid an actress as you are?"

Margot was evidently turning over a new idea in her head.

"But I must keep up my position. I can't be expected to wait while a lot of second-rate people go through a patriotic tableau and singing."

Beverley raised her shoulders.

"I don't know anything about that. I'm only looking at it from your children's point of view. They are too young to understand standing on dignity and things of that sort, they only know that all those people on the stage thought you were behaving badly, and they were ashamed."

Margot looked at Peter.

"You saw what happened. Do you think she's right?"

He left the wall and came over to her.

"Yes."

"What would you do? I can't bear them to feel like that about me."

"Let Miss Shaw take them home, and then go up and see them and try to explain."

"I think you're rehearsing your new play," Beverley broke in. "If you explained you were overtired because of that, I'm sure they'd understand."

Margot's eyes blazed.

"I don't need any advice from you. I can manage my own children."

"I'm sorry." Beverley opened the door. "I'll leave after breakfast tomorrow."

Peter gripped Margot's arm.

"Come on, be big. You can't let her go like that."

For a moment Margot wavered, then she went to the door and called up the passage.

"Miss Shaw."

Beverley turned.

"Yes."

"You needn't go, but don't let me have to complain again."

Beverley would have given almost anything to have said, "Thank you, but I'd rather go," but the children stopped her. She thought of Meggie's strained face, of Betsy's unexpected cry, "She's going to send you away," of David's wobbling, "You won't go away, will you, Shawskins?" Children so desperately needed secure backgrounds, and though she had not been with them long, that was what she created. In a house living on moods she stood for stability. She crushed down thoughts of herself and her pride and smiled politely.

"Thank you. It's very kind of you."

CHAPTER NINE

THE SUN WAS SHINING and it was a perfect spring day. Beverley sat up in bed and stared out of the window, her face lighting.

"Annie, I've had a marvellous idea." She got out of bed and dragged on her dressing-gown and slippers. "I'm going to telephone my friend, Sarah."

Sarah answered the telephone herself; Beverley kept her voice low so that none of the children in their bedrooms should hear what she was saying.

"I say, Sarah. If I can wangle permission and the car this end, would you bring the children for a primrosing picnic?"

Sarah's voice was a delighted squeak.

"I'm sure I can. Hold on while I ask Mrs. Elton." There was a pause, and then she came back bubbling with pleasure. "Yes, she'd be delighted."

"Good. Then, unless I ring you, we'll call for you at eleven, and we'll bring the lunch."

"I say, it's awfully good of Mrs. Cardew." Beverley laughed.

"You mean it will be awfully good of her; she doesn't know yet."

Beverley went back to her room and sat on the bed.

"Annie, I want to take the children out for a primrosing picnic, and I want the car, and I want lunch for eight, or rather nine, with the chauffeur."

"Don't want much, do you?" said Annie.

Beverley hugged her knees.

"It's such a lovely day, and it'll do them such a lot of good."

"I should say it's what they need after yesterday's trouble."

"That's just what I think."

Annie peered out of the window.

"I wouldn't half mind going primrosing myself. Get properly fed up with the streets this time of year." She turned round, smiling. "Listen to me carrying on. What you going to do about the car and that; ask Miss Winks?"

Beverley considered.

"I'd much rather see Mrs. Cardew. I wonder what time she wakes."

"Not very late. That Marcelle is generally kicking up a fuss over her breakfast-tray when I take our things down to the kitchen."

Beverley got off the bed.

"Good. I'll write a note, and you can give it to Marcelle to give her."

Annie shook her head.

"And have it pushed away under a plate or something where she can't see it. No, you write it now, and I'll slip into the hall and shove it in amongst her post."

Beverley had tactfully kept out of Margot's way when she had come up to see the children the night before, which made her the more anxious to see her personally this morning. Apart from the fact that, if Margot was still fairly vitriolic, she did not want her anger to fall on the

159

unfortunate Winkle, she was determined if she was going to stay on to establish a personal relationship. "It's a bit early to be tactful," she thought, getting out her writing-pad. "But here goes."

"Could I see you for a moment as early as possible? You told me it was your wish that the schoolroom routine should not be too hide-bound, but all the same, for a scheme I have for today, I should like your consent.

BEVERLEY SHAW."

Breakfast was over when Marcelle came up. Her face was very sour.

"Will you come down to Madame for a minute, Miss Shaw?"

Beverley held up a silencing hand to hush the children's nervous outcry.

"It's all right. I asked your mother to see me."

On the stairs Marcelle said:

"It is not good that Madame should be troubled so early."

Beverley raised her eyebrow.

"I don't think a few words about her children will overtire her."

Marcelle pursed up her lips.

"I am the one who can judge that. Always I have arranged who she sees."

Beverley hurried on.

"I'm sorry, but I really can't have you interfering over

160

the schoolroom affairs."

Marcelle laid her hand on her arm.

"I should not quarrel with me."

Beverley stood still.

"Really, Marcelle, what is the matter? I want to see Mrs. Cardew for a minute about the children, and you behave as if I were planning a murder."

Marcelle shrugged her shoulders.

"I know what I know."

Beverley had to laugh.

"I suppose you do. So do we all. But, you know, nothing you know, has anything to do with me."

She knocked on Margot's door.

Marcelle turned away.

"Very well. I know how we stand."

Margot was sitting up in bed having her breakfast. The eyes she turned on Beverley were like icicles.

"Yes, Miss Shaw?"

"Would you allow the children to come primrosing today?"

Margot wriggled back into her pillows.

"Why not? Why worry me with a silly question like that?"

"Because it's a very awkward day to ask you to give them a treat like that. It means our having your car and you have a matinée."

Margot reacted to this diplomacy.

"Oh, well, I can take a taxi. Mothers are used to making sacrifices."

"The other thing is, may those Elton children Miss

161

Winks spoke to you about come with us? They get very few treats, they are poor."

Margot looked vague.

"Children of a clergyman. Winkle knew of him." Beverley had an inward smile at Winkle's white lie.

"Well, I don't see why not."

"It's very good of you if you allow it. It's quite an undertaking bringing lunch for a party that size."

Margot, who was obviously very little rested after the night, ran a hand across her forehead.

"Well, I'm not exactly a beggar. See Winkle. She'll arrange it, and try in future not to worry me with needless questions."

"You mean picnics and so on with the Elton children are all right?"

"Yes, I've said so. Now do run away. I've got a headache."

Beverley went down to Winkle.

"I've seen Mrs. Cardew." She stopped Winkle interrupting with a gesture. "All right, don't fuss, I had to. She's got a headache and she's very nervy, but I wanted the car, and a picnic lunch for eight, and permission to do it again, so I had to see her myself."

"A picnic lunch for eight." Winkle drew the house phone to her, looking resigned.

"And the chauffeur. That makes nine."

Winkle groaned.

"Oh, dear, and the cook almost giving notice anyway. What time do you want the lunch and the car?"

"Ten forty-five."

It was not until Beverley had the whole party in the car, heading for Sussex, that she really believed they were off. She and Sarah were sitting side by side on the tip-up seats; Meggie and Miriam were in front; Betsy, David, Marjorie and Hannah packed in the back seat.

"How ill Meggie looks," said Sarah.

Beverley glanced over her shoulder, but the four behind were too deep in a noisy giggling game to bother with governesses.

"We had a bad day yesterday. I'll tell you afterwards. She's got one of her nervous headaches. She's feeling terrible, I'm afraid, poor child, but I thought on the whole primroses would be a better cure than bed."

Sarah leant sideways to look at Meggie's lolling head.

"Stop the car. You take Miriam in here with you. I'll do that child good."

"How?"

"I'll massage her head, I'm a dab at it. I bet you I send her to sleep."

The change was made. Sarah got in beside Meggie.

"I hear you've got a headache."

Meggie nodded feebly.

"Shawskins gave me some aspirin, and some stuff to drink, but I still feel awful."

"And look it," said Sarah cheerfully. Meggie was on the outside; she put her left arm round her and pulled her head on to her shoulder. "My mother has terrible headaches. We live in Bolton near some works. She says it's that. You know the twelve o'clock siren and all the smoke. Nothing like noise and smoke." She pressed her

163

fingers over Meggie's scalp, with untaught skill, picking out the aching nerves and tightened skin. "Often I massage her just like this. Funny I've never done it without sending her to sleep. She's a good relaxer, my mother is. She says directly she feels my fingers, she knows she's going to sleep."

Beverley, talking to Miriam, had half an eye on Sarah. She watched the swing of her shoulders as her fingers moved. Presently she saw they stopped moving, that she looked down at Meggie, then triumphantly over her shoulder her lips forming the word "Asleep."

They found a wood; it was full of stubby undergrowth and the white remains of trees that had been cut down. It was a mosaic with primroses. Great yellow patches amidst the wood anemones and dog's mercury. There was a little stream at the wood bottom, and there grew the long stemmed ones. The catkins were still on the trees, and the pussy willow was shining in the glory of its gold halo.

The children ran about calling to each other to come and look. There were violets under a woodpile. There was a bird's nest in the process of being built. There was an old hat that caused roars of meaningless laughter.

Beverley and Sarah spread the cloth and laid the lunch. Beverley looked happily at Meggie who, with Miriam, was crossing the stream by a very unsteady looking branch.

"She looks marvellous. I am grateful."

"Idiot. Look at my three. If there's any thanking to be done we owe it to you for thinking of asking us, and Mrs. Cardew for allowing us to come."

Beverley, unwilling to discuss Margot in such peace,

changed the subject.

"How's Mrs. Elton?"

Sarah sat on her haunches, a chicken in her hand half out of its greaseproof paper wrapping.

"Better."

Beverley was struck by her tone.

"Really better?"

Sarah nodded.

"The doctor told Mr. Elton yesterday that she's so much better that he thinks she ought to try leading a normal life soon."

Beverley glanced round at Miriam laughing as Meggie slithered about on the branch over the water; at Marjorie who, humming to herself, was solemnly picking a bunch of primroses; at Hannah who, with David, was crawling round the wood pile in search of a bird's nest.

"But you'll still stay?"

Sarah shook her head.

"No. For a bit of course. But, as soon as possible, I'm to go. As long as I'm there she'll never make a real effort."

"But they're like your own children."

Sarah gazed tranquilly through the wood.

"They are never one's own. I shall take on a new family."

Beverley unpacked a box of fruit.

"But you've been much more than a governess. They'll miss you terribly."

Sarah's face remained tranquil.

"I dare say. But Mrs. Elton is a splendid person. The best thing that could happen to them is that she gets all right, and, after all, what's best for them is what matters."

The early drawing in of the day sent them home early. The car bulged with primroses and branches of leaves, and David was clasping a matchbox in which was a caterpillar. It was with real regret that the Cardews parted with the Eltons.

"See you next Saturday," Miriam said to Meggie. "I'll ring you up."

"If you bring a lettuce leaf I'll give it to my caterpillar," David comforted Hannah, who had seen the caterpillar almost as quickly as David had and felt she had part claim to it.

Betsy leant out of the car window to speak to Marjorie.

"I don't promise, but I might let you wear my watch sometimes. I've had it for so many years the excitement has worn off."

"You people hungry for tea?" Beverley asked as the car moved off.

"Um," David grunted. "But first I've got to make a proper cage for my caterpillar."

"And somebody has got to put all these primroses and leaves in water," said Betsy.

Beverley laughed.

"And that'll be all of you."

"One would think that nobody was paid to do things for us," Betsy grumbled.

Beverley opened her eyes.

"What did I hear you say?"

Betsy reddened.

"Well, you know what I mean."

Beverley sighed.

"I was hoping the Betsy who made insufferable remarks of that sort was gone for good."

Betsy snuggled against her.

"So she has, Shawskins; but you will help me put mine in water, won't you?"

"Of course I will, we'll all do it together, it'll be fun, you'll see."

The last of the branches and flowers were arranged when the door opened and Peter looked in. His voice was less casual than usual.

"Can I come in a second? I told Mrs. Cardew I'd be here after her matinée."

Beverley looked at him in surprise.

"Of course."

"Dear me," he said, staring round. "All the country come to London."

Meggie put some sticky bursting chestnut buds on her bookcase.

"Birnam Wood has come to Dunsinane."

He laughed and patted the caterpillar's box.

"And what's come here?"

David, his eyes shining, lay across the table.

"It's my caterpillar. I've called him Cassius. You know, 'yon Cassius has a lean and hungry look.' He's going to be a crys'lis presently Shawskins says, and when he's finished being that he'll be a butterfly."

Annie came to the door and Beverley nodded to David.

"Time, old man."

David frowned.

"Oh, just five minutes. Peter's only just come."

Beverley caught hold of his legs and slid him off the table.

"You know what happens to anybody who says 'Just five minutes.' It's five minutes less tomorrow. Hop along and take Cassius with you. He can sleep by your bed. I'll be along in half an hour to tuck you up and hear your prayers."

David giggled.

"Will you tuck up Cassius and hear his prayers?"

Beverley nodded.

"I'll tuck him up, but he does his praying to himself."

David gave Peter a hug.

"I can just see him kneeling against a lettuce leaf with his eyes shut and all his legs folded."

Peter looked after David with an amused smile, then he turned to Beverley and opened his mouth as if he were going to speak, instead he closed it suddenly and shoved his hands in his pockets. He glanced awkwardly round the room.

"Oh, well . . . I suppose I ought to be going . . . I mean, mustn't disturb you . . . Well, I dare say Mrs. Cardew is back."

Meggie, Betsy and Beverley stared at the door as it shut after him.

"Gosh!" said Meggie, "what's the matter with him?"

Betsy skipped round the room.

"I think he's got a guilty conscience." Suddenly she stopped. "He can't have quarrelled with Mummy, can he?"

Meggie turned an anxious face to Beverley.

"Do you think it's that? He did seem in a fuss."

Beverley did not hear her. What was the matter with Peter? She longed to run after him and say "What is it? Is something worrying you?" She had positively to force her feet to stay where they were.

Meggie's eyes widened as she looked at her. Then she turned away.

"I expect it's nothing." She stroked the primroses which were in a bowl on the table. "Do you think I could have my supper in bed?"

Beverley pulled herself together.

"Of course. What's the matter, has your headache come back?"

"No." Meggie shook her head, her face looking rather scared. "No, it's just I'm tired."

Beverley washed and changed for her solitary supper, made her good-night round of the children. David scrambled off his bed at the sight of her, and hurried down on to his knees. She put her arm round him.

"You're in an awful hurry to say your prayers."

David nodded.

"It's pretty urgent. Annie says she had a caterpillar like Cassius and it ate too much and it burst. Can I do the asks first?"

"Very well."

"Dear God, bless Mummy, Meggie, Betsy, Shawskins, Annie and all in this house, and make me a good boy, and please, God, don't let Cassius burst, but if you must, please let him do it when I'm looking. Amen.

Jesus, tender Shepherd, hear me,
Bless Thy little lamb tonight.
Leave him alone and he'll come home
Bringing his tail behind him."

"David, you're not attending."

David opened his eyes.

"Not much I wasn't; I was wondering how the inside of a caterpillar looks. Of course, I don't want him to burst, but I can't help wondering."

"Well, don't wonder now. Start again."

Betsy was having her supper at a small table by her electric fire. She looked in an aggrieved way at Beverley.

"Is Meggie having her supper in bed?"

"Yes."

"Right in?"

"I expect so."

"Well, it's mean as mean. Here's me feeling utterly worn out and Annie won't let me have my supper in bed because she says I wouldn't get out again for my teeth."

Annie, who was arranging the bed, grinned.

"Neither would you, and well you know it."

"That's beside the point," Betsy argued. "The question is—will Meggie?"

Beverley kissed her.

"She will. Annie will remind her, won't you, Annie? Good night, Puss."

Betsy threw her arms round her neck.

"I do love you."

Beverley drew away from her, laughing.

"What's that leading up to?"

"Well, it's not so much leading up as getting you in a good mood in case it's fine tomorrow, because if it is I'd like to wear one of my new frocks and no coat."

Beverley looked across at Annie.

"You must tell her about not casting clouts till May is out." She patted Betsy's head. "If it's fine, very fine, perhaps a new frock, but under no circumstances no coat, so make your mind up to it."

Meggie was in bed; she gave Beverley a furtive little look.

"Had your bath?" Beverley inquired.

"Yes."

Beverley sat down on the bed beside her.

"It was lovely in that wood. I wish we could go every day."

Meggie nodded.

"But we've got it always. I shall always be able to shut my eyes and see it."

Beverley looked at her thoughtfully.

"There'll be such a lot of lovely things in your life. Are you going to try and make mental photographs of them all?"

Meggie took Beverley's hand and played with her fingers.

"I don't suppose that there'll be many when you're frightfully happy. I was so glad today I felt fat inside."

Beverley looked down at Meggie's long, lean fingers.

"I can't think why there shouldn't be thousands of times in your life when you're really happy."

"No." Meggie gave her head a violent shake. "I was thinking that in my bath just now. I don't mean ever to get fond of people any more. I mean not new people."

"Why?"

"Because being fond of them hurts. All the time you are being fond, you are frightened, at least I am."

"What of?"

"That something will happen. That they'll die, or be run over, or go away, or love somebody else instead of you."

Beverley thought for a moment; when she spoke she was not answering Meggie, but explaining things to herself.

"I think being hurt would be worth while."

Meggie tightened her hand round Beverley's.

"It wouldn't. I'm going to grow up trying not to love people too much."

"You'll be lonely, I should think."

Meggie shrugged her shoulders.

"I'll be too busy. An actress hasn't much time to be lonely."

The word "actress" brought Beverley's mind to Margot. Perhaps if Meggie had her mother's temperament to contend with it would be a help if she tried not to get too fond of people. She could still hear the suffering in Margot's voice as she heard it on Sunday night. She got up and kissed Meggie.

"Well, don't worry your head about loving people. It either happens or it doesn't. I don't think you can help yourself when it does."

Meggie started to answer.

172

"Can't—"

"Can't what?"

Meggie shook her head.

"No. I was going to ask you something, but I won't. Good night, Shawskins."

The telephone rang just as Beverley was going to bed; she answered, frowning. How inconsiderate of somebody to ring the house phone at such an hour—it might easily wake the children. It was Peter's voice which came over the wire.

"Is that you?"

"It's Beverley Shaw, if that's what you mean by 'you'. What is it?"

"You sound cross."

"Well, what an hour to ring up. You might easily have wakened the children."

"I'm sorry. I felt I'd left you a bit abruptly this evening. You'd wonder why?"

"I did, as a matter of fact. Is anything wrong?"

"No. It might be something right. What are your favourite flowers?"

"Mine?" Beverley's heart thumped. "Why?"

"I'd like to send you some."

"You can't do that. I mean, I'm just the governess and—" She broke off. He was being indiscreet enough on a phone on which it was possible anyone might be listening in, without her making things worse by saying, "and anyhow, Mrs. Cardew is in love with you, and would be livid if you sent flowers to her governess."

"I needn't send them to you. I can bring them for the

173

children. I thought of it tonight with all those primroses about."

Beverley decided that, pleasant though a present of flowers might be, the idea needed killing at birth.

"I haven't a favourite flower."

"You must like seeing one sort about more than another."

"No, I don't. I don't judge flowers by their looks, I go by their smell."

He chuckled.

"All right, good night. I like well-scented flowers myself."

Beverley put down the receiver and stood vaguely scaring at it. Her mind said, "This won't do. This is going to lead you into a horrible mess." But in her heart it was as if clouds were lifting off a new countryside of breath-catching beauty.

CHAPTER TEN

PETER AND BEVERLEY met at the Apèritif. They sat side by side at one of the wall-tables at the far end.

"How are the children?" he asked when he finished ordering the food.

"Very well. The matinée is safely over, thank goodness, and we're back at our usual routine."

"They looked very nice and kept still, and Margot spoke her stuff beautifully."

"You saw it?"

"Yes. I'd taken a couple of seats. Why, are you surprised?"

"Well . . . Oh, I don't know . . . I mean I . . . we haven't seen you about lately. The children were pleased with the roses. But you shouldn't have sent them. I told you not to."

He broke up a bit of toast Melba.

"I wanted to." There was an awkward pause which he ended by saying, "Here's our cocktails."

Beverley glanced round the restaurant.

"How nice everybody looks. It must be fun to have good clothes."

He eyed her in surprise.

"You couldn't look nicer."

Beverley sipped her cocktail.

"That's an awfully polite lie. I certainly could. My hat's new, I bought it this afternoon, but the rest is neat-outfit-provided-by-orphanage-suited-to-governess."

He put his head on one side examining her.

"I like that hat. It's not quite such a tomfool shape as most of the women are wearing."

She sighed.

"I wish it was. But those sort of shapes aren't suitable to governesses."

He paused while the waiter helped them to caviar.

"You know, you're one of those women who one never notices what they wear."

"I bet you would if I was well dressed. It's only because my clothes are what they are you don't. I'm protective-tinted like an animal."

There was another long silence. Suddenly he laid down his knife.

"I've always gone straight to the point, Beverley, and I'm going to do it now. I've fallen in love with you."

It seemed to Beverley that the chatter of the restaurant died and they were alone. She stared at him, her eyes growing wider and wider. While she looked she understood things. Why her heart jumped about when he came to see the children. Why she felt light-hearted just because he was in the house, even though she never saw him. Why since Saturday, his last visit, life had seemed colourless. When at last she spoke her voice was a whisper.

"Is it being in love when a person being about makes all the difference?"

He laid a hand on hers.

"It's a good start."

"When did you start loving me?"

176

"Probably the first time I saw you, but I didn't know it. I only knew it when you came into Margot's dressing-room, all your heckles up, looking like a mongoose."

"A mongoose!"

"Yes." He told her about the fight he had seen. "Silly, brave little beast."

"Me or it?"

"Both."

The waiter took away their plates and brought the next course. But they scarcely saw him. The wine waiter poured a little wine into Peter's glass and waited for him to taste it, but he never noticed, so with the shrug of one dismissing amiably the vagueness of lovers, the waiter filled both glasses and left them alone.

Beverley gave her head a puzzled shake.

"Have you changed, or am I looking at you differently? Quite suddenly you're not Mr. Crewdson, the children's friend, but—"

"Yes?"

She flushed.

"It seems so silly. People don't fall in love all in a minute like this."

"We have. What's it matter to us what other people do?" He ran his eyes lovingly over her face. "Shall I take another job abroad? There was talk about Kenya. You'd have room to expand there all right."

She lay back in her seat.

"The bark and the whine and the croaks, the crack of rotten branches broken under an animal's pad."

He nodded.

"What's it like? Is it silent? I always picture that part of Africa as feeling very big, and quiet like a cathedral, and a green, savage smell. You see, you aren't the only one who remembers conversations." He tapped her plate. "You haven't eaten a thing."

Obediently she finished her *Steak Diane*. The watchful waiter once more removed their plates and the sweet waiter pulled his wagon in front of them.

"I don't want any more, thank you," said Beverley. "Just some coffee. I feel much too odd inside to eat."

The coffee in front of them, Peter lit a cigarette.

"Do you think you could be happy married to me? We could settle down sometime in a not too fashionable place, with a garden which would be nice for kids, and—"

Beverley caught his arm.

"Good gracious. What am I thinking of? Sitting here in a kind of dream. I can't marry anybody just now, there's the children, and—" She hesitated, "and their mother."

His jaw set in a determined line.

"I saw all this would crop up. I expected it to crop up sooner. To take Margot first. I can't discuss it; she's been grand to me. But we're only friends."

Beverley played with her coffee spoon.

"I heard you the Sunday before last. You see, the door was open. I tried not to, but I couldn't help it."

He tapped some ash into the tray.

"She gets excited," he said at last. "Temperamental creature. Says a lot of things she doesn't mean."

Beverley looked up.

"If you want to marry me we must have things clear.

178

She's in love with you; it's no good pretending she isn't."

He looked embarrassed.

"Well, suppose she is; it'll wear off. I'm not her sort."

"She's in love with you," Beverley repeated, "and I don't know what she'd do if she knew about me."

"Well, she needn't know till you're out of the house. Just give in your notice or whatever governesses do."

Beverley sighed.

"You can be stupid. You a man with a job to talk like that. Do you generally throw up your job at a few minutes notice and walk out?"

He frowned. Looking, she thought, like a hurt, small boy.

"That's a different business."

She wanted most terribly to put her arm through his; it would have made explaining easier, but she could not do that in the restaurant. Instead, she looked at him, in the same way, and used almost the same voice she would use to David.

"It isn't a different business. Don't think I don't care; the more I look at you, the more I know I care terribly. But I've taken those children on, and tried to make them fond of me. I couldn't just walk out on them. When I go there'll be a lot of explaining to them, and I wouldn't go at all unless the right person were found to take my place."

"Listen, darling. I've got another fortnight only of this treatment. The doctors say I'm fit for anything in six weeks' time. I'd like to put in for that Kenya job. It'll only last about a year, and we can call it our honeymoon."

"Six weeks!"

He smiled.

"Too much of a hurry? Do you want longer to make up your mind?"

"No." Her voice was certain. "But it's arranging things at number ten. Mrs. Cardew is studying a new play; it's a rotten moment to upset her."

"You needn't worry about that side. I'll tell her."

She gave him a horrified look.

"No, you don't. You don't seem to have got on to what would happen. There would be the most awful scene which would upset the children terribly, and I won't have that."

"Well, someone's got to tell her."

"Not yet. I'll start working the children round to the idea of my going, and I'll see if the college know of someone to suggest to take my place, and then I'll give in my notice, and then I'll tell Mrs. Cardew."

"How long's all this going to take?"

She considered.

"A month, five weeks." She came to a decision. "You can put in for the Kenya job."

He gripped her hand so hard that it hurt.

"And you'll come with me?"

The thought of it was almost unbearable. The long sea voyage, the new country, the wildness, and the strangeness; all that she had ever wanted, and Peter, too.

"Yes."

Being in love changes your vision. Beverley thought she was looking and behaving exactly as usual, but nobody else thought so. One morning when Annie called her, she jerked back the curtains with a grunt.

"Raining cats and dogs."

Beverley sat up and looked at the leaden sky with dreamy pleasure.

"Oh, Annie, look what a lovely soft grey everything is."

Annie swung round and shook her head slowly and meaningly.

"So it is that."

Beverley spoke without moving her eyes from the sky.

"Is what?"

Annie made the proud sniff of one in the right.

"I was sure it was that. He'd the look and you'd the look. If there was anybody in this house I'd demean myself by taking a bet with, I'd have took it."

Beverley's face was scarlet.

"What are you talking about?"

Annie tapped her nose.

"Don't mind me. Secret as the grave I am. But I know the look. My mother has two half-sisters, only a year or two older than me. First it was Maudie. 'Whatever's come over Maudie?' my mother said. 'Looks properly queer. Hope she isn't going into a consumption.' My father laughed so I thought he'd burst. 'It's consumption of the heart then,' he said. And he was right. Three months later was the wedding."

"Well, but—"

"No good you arguing, Miss Shaw. Even if I hadn't all along spotted the way the wind was blowing I know the look now. So I ought. You should have seen Rosie, my mother's other half-sister; she got the same soft look you've had lately. I remember when it first took her, she was looking at our manure heap. 'Lovely colour, manure is,' she said. Then we knew. That's why I turned so quick when you came all poetic about a dirty morning."

"You mustn't talk like that, Annie," said Beverley, snatching at the threads of her dignity.

Annie shook her head and came over to the bed. Her voice was gentle.

"And why not? Because I'm common and you're a lady? Whether you're Queen of England, or a tinker woman, being in love feels the same. When it's going right we're all happy, and when it's going wrong we're all hurt just as bad."

Beverley gave up the hopeless task of silencing Annie.

"No one must know."

Annie opened her eyes.

"Are you stopping on then?"

"For a little, anyway. I can't walk out on the children all in a minute; besides—"

Annie lowered her voice.

"You take a tip from me. You give in your notice today. You don't know how you look, but if 'she' sees you, she'll spot what's happening quick enough and then heaven help you. If I was you I couldn't run quick enough or far enough."

Beverley got out of bed. She felt uneasy at Annie's words, but she managed to laugh.

"Don't be silly. Besides, you've no right to speak of Mrs. Cardew like that."

Annie handed Beverley her dressing-gown.

"Well, a cat can look at a king, so I expect I can look at Mrs. Cardew without shutting my eyes, and what I say is, run, before she finds out."

The children began to be curious. Peter no longer came to the house and so he wrote. The first letter arrived at breakfast-time. There was never much post for the schoolroom. A letter now and again for Annie, once in a while the children heard from their relations, or some friend sent them postcards, and Beverley occasionally got a letter from a school friend. Post was, of course, popular, and the owner of any form of correspondence was expected to share.

Bitterly Beverley regretted now her previous generosity in this matter. Every letter she had received she had shared. Small items of mild interest. "My friend Agnes is looking after twins." "A girl I was at college with called Norah is governess to some children in Australia and she says—" With discretion which she knew he must loathe as much as she did, Peter had typed the address. Ridiculous as it seemed even to her she knew who the letter was from even as Annie laid it beside her. The type meant nothing, the fact that it was a letter from Peter might just as well have been written across it. There was no other post that morning. The children stopped eating and glued their eyes on the envelope.

"Good. You've got a letter, Shawskins," said David.

"Open it quickly," Betsy demanded. "Perhaps it's about those twins who are the same age as me."

Meggie waited a moment and then she said in a strained

voice:

"Why don't you read your letter?"

Beverley was flustered. She disguised how she felt by taking a gulp of coffee. She knew Peter's hand-writing must be perfectly well known to all the children. It was possible that she could make something up for Betsy and David, but she would never fool Meggie. She laid down her cup.

"Sorry, but it's private."

Betsy had just helped herself to honey; she paused with the spoon dripping on to her plate.

"How can you know a letter's private before you've opened it?"

Beverley took the spoon from her and put it back on its plate by the comb.

"I was expecting it."

Betsy spread her bread thoughtfully.

"I do hate people who are secret over things. When we get letters everybody can read them."

David put down his mug of milk

"Is it a bad 'private'? Have you got mixed up in crime?"

Meggie had been staring at Beverley, now suddenly she turned on the other children.

"Shut up, both of you. I suppose she can have private letters if she wants to?"

Betsy's eyes twinkled.

"Of course she can, Meggie, dear. Can't you, my darling, adorable Shawskins?"

Beverley grinned back at Betsy.

"Yes, my beloved, delicious Betsy."

In her bedroom Beverley tore open the letter.

"BEVERLEY, MY DEAR,

This is a dismal way to live. I can't come to the house and you can only get out so seldom. Do go and make a clean breast of things to Margot, or let me. I'm sure she'll be understanding. Have you written to the college about finding someone to take your place? We ought, I think, to be doing something about getting our banns called. I spoke to Sir John Pilkin on the telephone; he's the man who really fixes the Kenya business. He says it's certain I can have the job if my doctor can give me an O.K. on the health side.

I am counting the minutes until Thursday. Take care of yourself for me, for you are all my life.

PETER."

Beverley kissed the letter and put it inside her frock. Even a letter was a little bit of him. She smiled at the phrase, "I'm sure she'll be understanding." How like Peter to think Margot would ever he understanding. It was being borne in on her the more she thought of it that Margot must never know about the engagement until she was out of the house and the new governess safely installed. If she knew, she might be so angry that she would refuse to have a governess from the same training college. All this writing about banns and Kenya made her worried. If only it was all settled and she had found someone nice to take her place. The trustful way the children looked at her, and the pathetic way they made

185

plans for the future, made her feel mean. What a pity
Sarah was not free. If only it had been a few months
instead of a few weeks she might have been.

"There's one thing you must do," she thought as she
went clown the stairs to the schoolroom, "and that is, to
take Winkle into your confidence. She'll have to do the
selecting of the governesses for Mrs. Cardew. Between us
we might find somebody perfect. And then I must have a
talk with Meggie."

Beverley went to Winkle after luncheon. It was the
children's dancing-class day and a good opportunity.

"Hullo, dear," said Winkle. "Pull up a chair. Will you
smoke?"

Beverley shook her head.

"No, I still haven't taken to it. No one can overhear us
in here, can they?"

Winkle looked startled.

"No, dear."

"Well, I need your help. I'm giving in my notice—"

Winkle eyed her in horrified surprise.

"Oh, no, dear! And you're doing so well. The children
are different people."

"It's because I'm going to be married."

"Married! Oh, my dear! Who to?"

Beverley swallowed.

"Peter Crewdson."

Not a sound came from Winkle for a full minute. Her
eyes seemed frozen with horror into one position. Her
mouth slowly opened and shut like a goldfish after an
ant's egg. When she at last got back her voice, it came out

in a Minnie Mouse squeak.

"Oh! Oh! Oh! But you can't. I mean, I don't know what will happen. I mean, Mrs. Cardew counts on him."

Beverley sighed.

"Don't I know. I can't think how he ever got himself jammed up with her, because, though he admires her frightfully, she's not the sort of person he'd think of marrying. He's awfully simple. I'm sure he'd be scared of her as a wife."

Winkle blinked and pushed her glasses down her nose.

"Oh, dear. I was afraid we were losing him when he stopped coming to the house. He hasn't been near us lately. But, of course, I never thought of you." She looked at Beverley reproachfully. "If I may say so, dear, haven't you been a little disloyal?"

Beverley leant forward.

"I keep wondering that. I do hope I haven't. I met him one Thursday in the park. We walked together." Unconsciously her voice took on the entranced tone of one repeating a fairy story. "He asked me to come to dinner with him the next Thursday. I said I would. I don't think I knew then I was fond of him, I only just knew I was glad to be talking to him. Then on the Saturday after the picnic he came up to the children. He was different then. He rang me up that night, and—oh, he was nice." She looked at Winkle candidly. "I suppose I could have said then I wouldn't see him on Thursday, but I couldn't."

Winkle blinked, and began clumsily to rearrange the papers in front of her.

"Dear, dear, dear. Most upsetting. When I was about

187

your age there was a young doctor. We were engaged. I had to break it off. My mother was ill and needed me." Her voice grew brisk, as if to kill a tendency to emotion. "And a very good thing, too, I am sure. I often say to myself, 'Now don't you go indulging in self-pity, Winkle. I'm sure you are better single.'"

Beverley longed to pat Winkle somewhere, but she was not sure she would like it. Instead she said:

"I'm sure you'd have made a splendid wife."

Winkle shook her head.

"Oh, no, dear. You know, often when I go home to my supper and am cooking myself a kipper or something, I look at it and say, 'It's lucky there's no man to grumble, that's very poorly served.' But the truth is, one hasn't heart for much, eating alone." She sat more upright and pushed her hands into her pockets. "Listen to me chatting of my silly little doings. Now, dear, what are you going to do?"

Beverley pulled her chair up to the desk.

"What I would like to do is to go straight to Mrs. Cardew." She held out a comforting hand to check Winkle's startled movement. "But I'm not going to. I want to get a new governess fixed for the children first, and then give in my notice. I want to make the change as easy for the children as possible. I don't mean I'm so important. Only, with all their schools and things, they've been so chopped about."

"You've gained their affection. It'll be very hard to replace you. I suppose that friend of yours, Miss Cox, isn't free?"

"That's the annoying thing. She will be fairly soon, but not soon enough. Peter and I are probably going to Kenya in about five weeks."

"Five weeks! Oh, dear, dear, dear!" Winkle pushed her glasses farther down her nose. "Oh, I do wish you could wait until after *Helen* is produced, it will be easier then."

"I can't. Peter's probably getting a year's job there. Anyway, I dare say it's a good thing she's busy. She's sure to leave choosing the new governess almost entirely to you."

"If only she doesn't learn about you. You've no idea what a state she's in already."

"Over the play?"

"No, over him. All day long she's ringing for me. 'Send a telegram.' 'Send this letter by messenger.' Such dreadful hysterics when he doesn't come." She dropped her voice. "I shouldn't say this, but I know you won't repeat it. She's drinking too much. She does when she's upset."

"I don't see why she should know until Peter writes and tells her, and he can save doing that until after the first night of *Helen*."

Winkle sighed.

"It sounds easy, but with people like Marcelle about you never know. Now about you. When do you want to leave?"

"At the latest a month from today. I've written privately to the principal of the training college, telling her I'm getting married and asking her if she can suggest a person to take my place. I've explained exactly what is wanted, and some of the difficulties of running a

189

schoolroom in this house. If she sends anyone, could you see them? Afterwards, perhaps, I could meet them."

Winkle got up and walked over to the window.

"Meggie will be a difficulty. She's devoted to you, and she is so like her mother in some ways."

"Yes." Beverley joined Winkle at the window. "I was so pleased when she got to like me. She seemed to need affection. She's been a lovely person to teach; every day I see her coming out more. It's been like watching a tree come out in the spring. Now I'm afraid. I'll never forgive myself if she feels I've deserted her, and is driven back into her shell."

Winkle fidgeted awkwardly with the curtain cord while she tried to bring herself to say what she wanted.

"Meggie will be all right. We'll manage. In any case, don't let us here upset you. Of course, all I was telling you about Eddie—that was his name—and myself, is a long time ago, but I remember those days quite well enough to think it a sin to let anything spoil the happiness of two people in love."

It was after tea when the azalea came. The envelope tied on to it just said, "For the nursery." Inside it had Peter's card, with scrawled across it, "Something with a nice smell for you all." It was a gorgeous plant, flame coloured, covered in sticky buds. Betsy and David admired it enormously.

"I wish, though, he'd said when he was coming," David said.

Betsy sniffed the scent.

"I believe Mummy's had one of her rows. He hasn't been here for weeks and weeks and weeks."

"Not as long as that," Beverley laughed. "He was here that day we went primrosing."

"Well, it seems weeks," Betsy argued. "Our lives are very dull just now, with Mummy working and never being in to see us after tea, and no cocktail parties or anything."

Meggie had scarcely glanced at the plant, but had gone with hunched shoulders over to the fireplace.

"You ought to put it in your bedroom, Shawskins," she growled without looking round. "It's a present to you, really."

Betsy and David stared at her.

"Peter's our friend," David protested.

Betsy glanced at Beverley, who had, to her annoyance, flushed.

"And he's Mummy's," she said slowly. She came up to Beverley and put her arms round her waist, and stared up at her. "Is it a present for you? And were the roses and the carnations?"

Beverley had to make a quick decision. She could not absolutely deny that they were for her, because when the children knew the truth they would he shocked at her telling a lie. On the other hand, she could not tell the truth; it would need tact in telling Meggie, and Betsy and David were unreliable with a secret. She planned a middle course.

"They were partly for me. He said he would like to send flowers for this room and he asked me what kind I liked,

191

and I said anything that smelt nice."

"That's the worst of grown-ups," David complained. "They always ask somebody else what presents we'd like instead of asking us that the present is for."

Betsy kept her eyes on Beverley's face.

"When d'you see him that we don't? I mean, when did he ask you about flowers?"

Meggie swung round.

"Shut up! Shut up! Shut up! Asking and asking. It's much better not knowing some things."

"I won't shut up," stormed Betsy. "I've as much right to her as you have."

In the uproar they none of them heard the door open. They were startled when Margot's voice broke in:

"What is this nasty noisums? Here's poor Mummy slipped away from rehearsal to see her babykinses, and she wants to see smiles." She came into the room and stopped at sight of the azalea. "What a lovely plantums. Where did you get that?"

There was a second's pause while Meggie and Betsy eyed each other, then Betsy blurted:

"Peter sent it."

Margot stiffened, her eyes took on their icy look.

"You little idiots. That plant was sent to me. How dare you touch it?"

"It wasn't, Mummy" David foraged in the paper-basket and brought out the envelope the card came in. "Look, it says 'for the nursery.' "

Margot took the envelope from the child and stared at it. For one awful moment Beverley thought she was going to cry, but she controlled herself, and made her voice casual.

"Has he sent you flowers before?"

David looked desperately at his sisters. Betsy, obviously nervous, stammered:

"Yes. Twice. Roses and carnations, things that smell." She stood on one leg, hoping for an inspiration. "They aren't sent to us, really, they're for Shawskins. He asked her what she liked, and— ough." She grabbed her ankle in both hands. "You kicked me, Meggie. You are a beast, it hurt."

Margot bent and smelt the flowers. Her face when she raised it was a mask; it showed absolutely no feeling of any kind. Without a word she turned and almost ran out of the room.

CHAPTER ELEVEN

M<small>ARGOT</small> went into her bedroom and rang for Marcelle. She nodded at the door as she came in.

"Shut that." Marcelle obediently shut it, and stood respectfully in front of it. "What do you know of the friendship between Miss Shaw and Mr. Crewdson, Marcelle?"

Marcelle wet her lips with her tongue. This was what she had been waiting for.

"Nothing, Madame." With skill she made the inflexion sound like, "Nothing I'm telling you."

Margot was used to Marcelle.

"Don't be tiresome. What do you want? Is it my fox cape that you are always pretending is getting shabby?"

Marcelle gave an expressive shrug.

"For a lady in the position of Madame, it is shabby; for me it will do very well."

Margot frowned, knowing she was being cheated out of a perfectly good fur cape.

"Oh, very well. Now get on with it."

Marcelle crossed the room, very conscious of the drama of the situation.

"It is now some weeks since I first suspect what is going on. It was that Sunday morning when you were taking Monsieur Crewdson to lunch in the country; you said to me, 'Marcelle, go and find Mr. Crewdson, he will be in the schoolroom perhaps, with the children.' I go up and knock on the schoolroom door, and what do I see?

194

Monsieur Crewdson kissing the governess." No words could describe the scorn that Marcelle put into the word "governess".

Margot was revolted.

"Kissing!"

"But yes, Madame, but that is not all. Disgusted at what I have seen I gave my message and came back to you, Madame, but when I reached the bottom of the stairs Monsieur Crewdson is after me. 'See, Marcelle,' he says, offering me a pound note, 'this is for you.' 'Monsieur,' I said, looking him very straight in the eye, 'you cannot bribe me to silence. I do not want your dirty money,' and I came straight to you, Madame."

"I wish you'd stick to the truth," said Margot. "I know perfectly well that if there was any money about you took it, and you know that I know. He paid you, did he?"

Marcelle flushed.

"All the gentlemen give me tips."

"I see. So he did. Now go on."

"After that it is always the same thing. Monsieur Crewdson, I think, does not wish to continue, but that governess she is a sly one, always waiting on the stairs and in the passage, and when she sees Monsieur Crewdson, her lips pouting so"—Marcelle gave a magnificent performance of a voluptuous woman. "I know the type. *Canaille!*"

"Anything more?"

"Then one night," Marcelle lowered her voice dramatically, "when Madame is at the theatre—quite late it is—the telephone bell rings. It is a call for the governess. The servants are very stupid, they think nothing, they put that call through to the schoolroom floor, but for me, I say, 'This concerns Madame. I should listen.' "

"Yes?"

"It is Monsieur Crewdson. He just rings up to know how the children enjoy their day in the country, but that governess, she takes the call to herself. 'Oh, the lovely primroses,' she says, 'I adore flowers.' What can Monsieur do? He promises that he will send more. Three times he has sent, roses, carnations, and today an azalea in a pot."

"And why," asked Margot, "have you kept all this to yourself?"

Marcelle gave a terrific shrug of her shoulders.

"Why distress Madame? It is impossible that that little governess can distract Monsieur for long. Madame has everything. I say to myself, 'My Madame is beautiful, she is great, she is rich, why disturb yourself? If Madame is good enough to interest herself in Monsieur Crewdson, then he will be interested.' That governess, she means nothing"—Marcelle snapped her fingers to show how little Beverley meant—"but nothing at all."

Margot marched up and down her bedroom thinking.

"I wonder?" She questioned herself more than Marcelle. "I wonder if that's what's keeping him from the house. If he's embroiled with the little wretch and doesn't quite know how to get out of it. It might be the reason."

"It might be," Marcelle agreed.

Margot paced angrily up and down.

"Don't stand there shrugging your shoulders and

agreeing with me. Go and get me a brandy. I feel like hell."

Marcelle went to the cabinet where the drinks were kept, and took out the brandy decanter. She poured Margot out a small glass. Margot, with an impatient look, crossed the room and dragged the decanter from her.

"I want a drink, you fool, not a sip." She half filled the glass.

Marcelle eyed her anxiously. She could do quite a lot with Margot in the ordinary way, but very little when, as now, she was encouraging herself with drink.

"It is time for Madame to eat before the theatre," she suggested cautiously.

"All right. Have you ever known me affected by drink? I could act if I drank bottles of this stuff."

Marcelle went to a cupboard and quietly took out Margot's outdoor things. She looked at her watch.

"I think that Madame's meal will be on the table."

Margot tipped back the brandy and looked at the clock.

"Blast! So it is. But I'll have it out with that little wretch tonight. Marcelle, you go straight up to Miss Shaw and tell her from me that she is not to go to bed, will she please be waiting in the nursery when I come in."

Beverley tried to sew, but she had one eye almost permanently on the clock. She had no illusions about her coming interview with Margot. All her thoughts how, if forced to tell the truth, to do it most kindly, and in such a way as not to cause her to be thrown out of the house in the morning. Almost she had confided in the

197

children before they went to bed. There was no mistaking Margot's face when she went out of the children's sitting-room. She was furious; it was practically certain she would say something. Beverley had held back from telling the children for the fear of upsetting them unnecessarily; it was ridiculous to blurt out now that she was leaving if, after all, she could stave things off for a few days. Tick, tock, went the clock; it seemed to her that time was passing very slowly. It was eleven o'clock. If Margot came straight home from the theatre, she got in before a quarter to twelve. She wished her heart did not beat so. "You are the most miserable coward," she thought. "You're terrified of seeing her. Your knees are like jelly; do have some guts, my girl."

It had been all she could do the whole evening to keep herself from ringing up Peter, and telling him what had happened. But that would be burning her boats with a vengeance. He would never allow her to have this row alone; he'd have been sure to have wanted to come round, and how she would have adored to have had him. Even imagining he was there put strength in her heart. What would there be to fuss about, when all she would have had to have done would have been to have slipped her hand into his and said, "Of course he sends me flowers, you see we're engaged to be married." She did not quite know what Margot would do if she was forced to say those words, but she did know, if ever there was a time in her life when she would be glad of someone to lean on, it was now.

"A quarter past eleven," she thought. "She ought to be

back in half an hour. Oh, dear, I do wish Marcelle hadn't looked so knowing, and I do wish she hadn't come in when Meggie was having her supper. I did my best, but I'm certain she was worried, poor child." She folded her work and put it back in her basket. "I think I'll go and powder my nose and do something to my hair. I'll feel twice as brave if I'm not looking too awful."

Beverley's bedroom door had barely shut when Meggie's was gently opened. She looked right and left up the passage, then pulling her dressing-gown tightly round her, she sidled towards the sitting-room with her back to the wall. When she reached it, with a nervous eye over her shoulder towards Beverley's door, she softly turned the handle and slipped in.

For all Beverley's efforts to make the nursery more of a sitting-room, it still looked like a modern nursery; it had extraordinarily few places in which even a person as small and thin as Meggie could hide. Sitting up in bed, straining to hear a movement in the passage, she had gone over in her mind what she meant to do. She was, practically convinced that Beverley and Peter were fond of each other. With all the passionate jealousy in her nature she resented the thought. Her life had been so chaotic, with her temperamental mother, her constant changes of school, and finally the disappearance of the one person she could trust, her nurse, she had got herself tied in a mental knot. With the coming of Beverley the knot had slowly untied. The small frictions of her child's world had gradually been smoothed out and the nervous dreads which had been part and parcel of her life died a natural death in the simplicity and routine that Beverley introduced. Nobody in Meggie's life had ever treated her with the understanding that Beverley had given her, and it felt to the child, warming and blossoming in the new atmosphere, that she had come out of a rough sea into a harbour. Fear that her mother would dismiss Beverley was always with her, but it was not till the night of the picnic that fright that she might have to put out to sea again because of Peter struck her. Trained to the theatre, over sensitive to emotional atmospheres, she had sensed the difference of feeling between Peter and Beverley, and hated it. But tonight she had a new emotion—fear.

With all the fastidiousness of her nature, she had disliked the sight of her mother fawning over Peter; she had fiercely denied in public that she was interested in him, but mentally she had never been misled. She knew that her mother wanted to marry him and feared that she would marry him, even if Peter himself did not want it. That was why she was afraid when she had heard her mother's message tonight. In a childish way she felt protective. She knew what her mother could be like when she was really angry. Beverley did not. If her mother was coming up to the nursery to have a row, she must be there to help Beverley.

In her bed, considering the sitting-room, she had decided there was only one possible place in which she could hide, that was behind the curtains. She would bulge a little, but perhaps they would not notice. Quiet as a cat she climbed up on the window-seat, pressed her back against the window, and let the curtains fall as nearly into

200

place as possible.

Margot had gone through the evening performance in a dream. Something in her refused to let her believe that the affair between Peter and Beverley was as negligible as Marcelle had made out. As an actress she had studied character, and neither Peter nor Beverley fitted in with Marcelle's story. When she was actually on the stage she was able more or less to kill the nagging fury in her heart, but in the dressing-room it took full possession of her. Mrs. Brown had an awful night. Nothing was right; she was cursed for everything she did and touched. Jealousy hurt Margot physically. She felt battered and bruised with pain and to kill it she resorted to more and more brandy. Mrs. Brown eyed her with despair.

"Got a good mind to ring up that nasty Marcelle," she thought, "and tell her to see 'she' gets straight to bed. Did ought to have a doctor really. Don't know when I saw her in such a state. It's that Mr. Crewdson. I wish he'd come round again. What with him, and her rehearsing that nasty murderess, something will happen if we're not careful."

The moment the curtain was down, Margot dashed for her dressing-room.

"I shall go home in my make-up, Brownie. I'm tired. I'll take it off in my bedroom. Give me my things."

Mrs. Brown, pulling off Margot's stage dress and helping her into her frock, kneeling on the floor while she changed her stockings and put on her shoes, was frightened to notice that she was unconscious of her. She sat and stood stiffly, her lips moving in a ceaseless mutter.

201

"It gives me the creeps," thought Mrs. Brown. "Looks as though she was having a row with someone."

Contrary to her usual custom, Mrs. Brown saw Margot out of the stage door and into her car. Then she went to the door-keeper.

"Put us a call through to Miss Dale's house, ducks."

The door-keeper nodded.

"Don't like the look of her," he said while he dialled the number.

He and Mrs. Brown were old friends. They said things to each other they would never have confided in anybody else in the theatre.

"Carried on alarming she has tonight. I'm getting on to Marcelle."

The door-keeper made a face over the receiver.

"That's a nasty bit of work."

Mrs. Brown nodded.

"Shocking." She took over the receiver. "Is that you, Miss Marcelle? This is Mrs. Brown speaking. I felt kind of worried about Miss Dale. I thought I'd give you the tip. I'm not sure she didn't ought to see a doctor."

There was impertinence in Marcelle's voice as it came over the wire.

"I do not think you need worry. There was a little trouble before Mrs. Cardew came to the theatre tonight. She will settle it when she comes in. It will do her good."

Mrs. Brown handed back the receiver to the door-keeper.

"It's lucky for that Marcelle, there's no getting at people through these things. Because I don't mind telling you I'd

202

have spat down it."

"What did she say?"

Mrs. Brown looked serious.

"Had a row with someone at the house. From what I can gather she's going to finish it when she gets in. I'd have a ten to one bet who the row's with, and I wouldn't be in her shoes for something."

Beverley, with her ears strained to catch the slightest sound, heard Margot's steps coming up the stairs. As usual in moments of crisis, she threw back her shoulders and lifted her chin to face it. Margot came in, closed the door behind her, and sat down at the table. She had had another drink when she got to the house, and was drunk without showing the slightest sign of it, only her face was haggard under her make-up, and her pupils twice their natural size. Her brain, lit by alcohol, was clearer than usual. She said nothing for a moment, but tapped the table with her fingers, then she looked up.

"Miss Shaw, I understand from some information that I have received, that you have been having a flirtation with a friend of mine."

Beverley flushed.

"Not a flirtation."

Margot held up her hand.

"Please don't interrupt. A vulgar, sordid little flirtation, kissing behind doors, and so on, and whispering rubbish over telephones. All of which you have done up here in my nurseries, probably without even troubling to hide it from my children."

"Look here," said Beverley, angry at the slur on her

professional dignity. "You're talking absolute rot. I must explain."

"I don't want any explanation. There are plenty words for you and your type, but I'm not going to bother to use them. I have the lowest opinion of people who disguise one profession under cover of another. You will pack your things tonight, and leave first thing in the morning, and I'm giving orders that you are not to see my children before you go."

Beverley looked at Margot in despair. How was it possible to talk to someone quite so unreasonable? She made her voice very gentle.

"Of course I'll pack tonight, but please let me see the children before I go. Things aren't like you imagine a bit. I was going to tell you, anyway, presently. I think you must be talking about Peter—"

"Peter!" Margot trembled. "How dare you!"

"But that's just it." Beverley's tone was as kind as she could manage. "He is Peter to me. You see, we love one another. We're going to be married."

It seemed to Margot that she had a violent blow between her eyes. For a moment her mind went a complete blank and stars danced in front of her eyes. When she saw clearly again she had lost all control of herself, and had no idea what she was doing. She got up from the table and came over to the fireplace where Beverley was standing; her voice was a whisper.

"That's a lie."

"No—" Beverley faltered a little before what she saw in Margot's eyes. "No, it's true. Oh, do believe me when I say

I didn't mean it to happen. It just did. It's all had to be rather hurried because he's getting a job in Kenya and we're going out there in about five weeks."

"You dare to tell me this." Margot spoke in whispered gasps. "You come into my house and you sneak round and you deliberately set out to steal the man I love. But you shan't do it. I don't care what happens, but you shan't do it." On the words, her hands sprung up and she forced Beverley backwards over the fireguard. It was a cold night and Beverley had kept up a good fire, which was now red-hot coals. "I'll rub your face in those coals. I'll make you look such a fright no man will ever want to marry you."

Margot had naturally strong hands, and what she had drunk had turned her into a maniac with a maniac's strength. In any case, Beverley was in a wretched position to offer resistance; she was half over the fireguard before she even suspected what Margot was thinking of doing. She did utter one cry, but it was confused by the noise as she and the guard fell over together. Fortunately, she fell sideways with her head towards the coal scuttle away from the grate.

"Going to Kenya, are you?" Margot muttered, dragging her by the neck towards the bars. "You'll look pretty when I've done with you. Just the kind of bride a man would choose—"

"Mummy!"

Margot turned more in annoyance at feeling the pull on her left arm than conscious that it was her daughter Meggie. Beverley took advantage of the momentary distraction and wriggled herself partially free.

"No, you don't." Margot pounced back at her.

Beverley, wrestling, managed to catch Meggie's scared eyes. She could only speak in a throttled gasp.

"Annie."

Annie was a deep sleeper, and it took a second or two to awaken her, but awake, she had only to hear a few words of Meggie's hysterical story, and without waiting for any such flapdoodles as dressing-gowns, she was flying up the passage on her bare feet. She was just in time; Beverley, hampered by the fireguard, and being on her back, was within an inch of the grate. Annie took it all in in a glance. She made a pounce at Margot and flung her arms round her.

"Good gracious, Mum, whatever's come over you? You can't be well. You ought to be in bed. Miss Meggie, dear, you run down to Marcelle, tell her your mother isn't well."

Beverley got up feeling bruised and shaken; without a word she picked up the fireguard and put it crookedly in its place. With the feel of Annie's arms round her the strength went out of Margot and sanity returned. She gave a gasp.

"My God! What was I doing?" Then she looked at Beverley. "But you told me—But it isn't true? Tell me it isn't true."

Beverley signalled to Annie to sit Margot in a chair.

"Don't let's discuss it any more tonight. You ought to be in bed."

Quite suddenly, Margot buried her head in her hands and began to cry, frightful, gasping sobs. She was like that when Marcelle came in. Marcelle looked round; she took in the crooked fireguard, the coal smears on Beverley's face, and on Margot's hands. She gave a grim smile. She made a gesture with her thumb to Annie.

"Take one of her arms, and I'll take the other, and get her down to her room. I'll ring up the doctor."

As the three of them went out, Beverley suddenly found that the place was swimming. She fumbled her way to a chair, and put her head between her knees. For a few seconds she passed right out. She was just returning to consciousness when Annie, by now in her dressing-gown and slippers, came back.

"Oh, my goodness!" said Annie, "you'd better lie down. Come on, Miss Shaw, dear. You lie flat on the floor here, and I'll bring some brandy; there's a little bottle in the medicine cupboard."

Beverley, too weak to resist, lay flat on the carpet. Bells rang in her ears, she felt sick. In a few minutes Annie was back and raising her head to a tumbler.

"There, drink this. You'll soon be all right."

The brandy pulled Beverley together; in a moment or two she got limply to her feet and crawled into an armchair.

"She was trying to murder you," said Annie, in an awestruck tone.

Beverley shook her head.

"No. She was just hysterical." She thought with a shudder how near she had been to the coals. "But she would have burnt me if—" She sat up. "Oh, my goodness, where's Meggie?"

"Gone back to bed, I should hope. That was a nice thing for a child to see."

Beverley got up.

"I must go to her. She'll be terribly upset, poor child."

Annie put her arm round her.

"Well, don't fall over. You're as wobbly as one of my mother's jellies." She led Beverley into the passage, and opened Meggie's door. Then she gave a gasp. "My! She isn't here." The two of them looked in a stunned way at the room. On the floor were Meggie's white satin pyjamas and blue quilted dressing-gown and slippers. Fright pulled Beverley together.

"Look and see which of her clothes are missing."

Annie dashed to the cupboards and pulled them open.

"Her white fur coat. I can't see anything else." She pulled open a drawer. "Yes, her blue shorts and jersey she uses for her exercises."

Beverley got down and looked in the shoe cupboard.

"Have any shoes gone?"

Annie glanced up and down the rows.

"Yes, a pair of brown." She looked over at the chair where she had folded the clothes the night before. "She didn't have time to put on any under-things; her combies are still here, and her stockings.

Beverley ran to the door.

"Come on, she can't have gone far."

The front door was ajar. Beverley and Annie ran down the steps into the street. It was absolutely empty. On their left was all the traffic of Piccadilly, on their right a few belated cars going up Curzon Street, but in all Way Street nothing was moving.

"Oh, my!" Annie moaned. "Where could she have run to this time of night, with no combies or stockings? She'll catch her death of cold."

Beverley clasped her hands, forcing herself to think clearly.

"It's no good going to her mother; she's in too much of a state to help anybody." Suddenly she knew what she must do. She turned and ran back into the house. "I'll get hold of Mr. Crewdson."

CHAPTER TWELVE

IT SEEMED to Beverley that as Peter came in through the front door the atmosphere of the house changed. Pacing up and down the hall waiting for him she had been as near to having hysterics as she was ever likely to get. To have allowed Meggie to run away. "It was criminal stupidity," she told herself, "and it's no excuse to say you were upset and forgot about the children. A decent governess does not forget about her children no matter what happens. Besides, you could have guessed something like this would happen. You understand Meggie, you know how sensitive she is. Imagine the effect on her of seeing her mother behaving like that."

She was still mentally showering shame on herself when Peter arrived. She had planned to take him into the little sitting-room where she had waited to see Margot the day she was engaged, and there quickly and concisely tell him what had happened, but her feelings got the better of her. He looked so normal, so utterly his composed usual self that without thinking at all she flung herself into his arms, calling out, "Peter. Oh, Peter," and burst into tears.

Peter, what with one thing and another, was used to crises; he took this one in his stride. In no time he had the rough details.

"Shorts and a jersey, bare legs, brown shoes, an ermine coat," he said to Annie.

"That's right, sir. But not her hat, nor her combies, nor her gloves, nor her stockings. I shouldn't wonder if she caught her death of cold, poor little mite."

He had put Beverley to sit on the stairs. Now he looked down at her smiling.

"She's a very intelligent kid of twelve. I shouldn't describe her as a mite. And it's April and quite warm. Had she any money with her, do you know?"

Beverley and Annie looked at each other in shame.

"How stupid of us," Beverley said, getting up. "I never looked. She's got a moneybox; I don't know if she took it. I'll go and see."

Peter caught hold of her.

"No hurry. We can't do a thing before the doctor comes down. If her mother is well enough she will have to decide whether we are to ring up Scotland Yard or what. As a matter of fact it won't surprise me if a policeman marches her home any minute; a hatless child with an ermine coat and bare legs is likely to be noticed trotting about London after midnight." He turned to Annie. "Do you think you could make a pot of tea? I think a cup would do us all a bit of good, and I dare say the doctor will know what to do with one when he comes down."

Annie beamed.

"Oh, yes, sir. I'll have one up in no time. Nothing like tea. My mother always says it'll see you through anything, whether it's a death or a birth."

As Annie disappeared in the direction of the kitchen, Peter gave Beverley a little shove.

"Move up, selfish. What's a nice step for if not for two." He put his arm round her. "I think you're fussing too much, you know. I always think when you're in a spot of bother it's a good thing to get all the dangers listed and give them a look over. There are two here, the first that she falls into the hands of some beast of a man, and the second that she gets run over."

"Well, isn't that enough?"

"I don't see there's any danger of either happening. Meggie's an intelligent kid; I'd trust her to fight her way out of most situations. Besides, London isn't littered with foul-minded males on the wait for little girls. As for being run over, you can count that practically out. She's been taught how to cross a road presumably."

"Of course. But she'll be in such an awful state; it's that I'm afraid of. She might do anything."

"What do you mean by 'anything'? Jump in the river?"

Beverley nodded.

"I wish I knew how much she'd heard. I can't help being afraid she must have been in the room all the time. If she wasn't, I don't see why she should have run away. She trusts me. I think it must have been hearing I was going which finished things; she would feel she had no one to turn to."

"What exactly did she hear her mother say to you? You didn't go into that."

"It wasn't so much saying as doing. She came up after tea and saw your azalea, and when she heard you'd sent it she said it was meant for her. The children had been arguing about whether it was a present for them or for me and Betsy lost her head and told her mother that it was mine. Afterwards I got a message from Marcelle to wait up and see Mrs. Cardew when she came in."

"Did Meggie know you'd got that message?"

"Yes, it came while we were at supper. I thought she looked upset."

"Well, what happened?"

"I waited, and then Mrs. Cardew came home. She thought, or said she thought, the most loathsome things, and she gave me my notice and told me I wasn't to say good-bye to the children. That seemed so awful that I risked telling her the truth. That was when she went queer." She gave a shiver, and his arm round her tightened.

"What happened, darling?"

"She tried to push me into the fire."

"What!" He got up, looking as if he were prepared that minute to climb to Margot's room.

"Not to kill me. She wanted to disfigure me, but honestly she didn't know what she was doing." She looked up. "Oh, don't look like that."

Peter hardly seemed to hear her. All in a flash, not only his face, but his whole body had changed. Every line on his face had hardened, and each muscle in his body had contracted, but it was his eyes which made the real difference. Ordinarily, he had eyes which, whatever he was saying, had a laugh at the back of them. There was no laugh anywhere near them now, and the difference it made was frightening. There was disillusion in them, but far more there was almost uncontrollable rage. She caught hold of his arm.

"She's ill. The doctor's with her, and honestly I'm not hurt."

He looked down at her hands.

"When I think what might have happened. Blind, idiotic fool that I was to leave you in this house. But—oh, I don't understand women, I suppose. My God, I wish she was a man."

"It's a very good thing she's not," Beverley said more lightly than she felt, "or we'd never get to Kenya. From the look of you, there'd be a trial for manslaughter."

"There would." His voice was so grim it silenced her. They stood a second without speaking, she feeling for the calming thing to say, he struggling to get control of himself. As a boy he had been given to bursts of flame-like temper; through the years he had not so much got rid of the attacks as beaten them down. Now it seemed that a crushed temper could grow underground. He had a wild longing to get hold of Margot by the throat and shake her so that he could hear her teeth rattle. His Beverley, his exquisite, simple Beverley to have been treated like that.

There was a step on the stair; Doctor Grey was coming down.

"How is she?" Beverley asked.

"Can I see her for a minute?" said Peter.

The doctor looked at him curiously.

"No. Nobody can see her. I've given her some stuff to quieten her, and I've got her a nurse." He nodded in the direction of the drawing-room. Suppose we go in there. Before I got Mrs. Cardew off I heard a good deal about you two." He looked at Beverley. "What happened exactly?"

"That woman wants horse-whipping," said Peter.

Beverley stamped her foot.

"Do shut up about her. She doesn't matter and I don't matter. It's Meggie."

The doctor stopped.

"Meggie! What's the matter with her?"

Beverley told him as quickly as she could what had happened, with great difficulty silencing Peter's explosive comments. In her face as she finished was pleading. Her eyes said clearly, "Do calm him down, and let's all fix our minds on what to do about Meggie."

As they reached the drawing-room, Annie came staggering along under an immense tray on which was not only a large pot of tea, but a loaf and a piece of cheese.

"Having it in here?" She planted it on a table. "It's the kitchen pot; all that silver looks nice, but there's nothing like a brown earthenware for flavour." She looked at Peter. "You see Miss Shaw drinks a cup, and try and get a bit of bread and cheese down her, she needs it." She turned to Beverley. "I'm just going up to my room to put on a coat and a pair of stockings. It's parky hanging about in a dressing-gown. I'll have a look in Miss Meggie's room while I'm up and see if she took her money-box."

Beverley stopped her.

"Have some tea first, it'll warm you." She got up to pour out, but Peter pushed her into a chair.

"You sit still. I'll see to this."

Doctor Grey walked up and down, his hands in his pockets.

"I wonder if the invaluable Winkle is on the telephone. She's the person we want. She would know where the

215

child might have gone and if we should try possible people first or ring Scotland Yard."

Beverley took her cup from Peter.

"Marcelle will know."

The doctor's face was grim.

"We'll have her down. I want a word with her, anyway." He gave a nod at Annie. "You'll call her?"

Annie gulped her tea and made for the door. Running about and making tea she had been unconscious of her clothes. Now, in the drawing-room, a room she had never before entered, let alone sat in, she felt self-conscious; her old flannel dressing-gown and slippers were all right, but not what she cared to he seen in with two gentlemen in the room. Grateful for an excuse, she hurried out.

Marcelle stood in the doorway, her face the very picture of what a maid-much-concerned-about-mistress should look. Doctor Grey, however, was not easily fooled by expressions; his voice was curt.

"Is Miss Winks on the phone?"

"Yes, sir. The number is on a card in the left hand drawer of her desk. Shall I telephone and tell her to come?"

"No." The doctor looked at Peter. "Perhaps you would, Crewdson?" He waited until the door was closed and then turned back to Marcelle. "You knew the state Mrs. Cardew was in when she come back from the theatre tonight!"

Marcelle's face was shocked.

"Oh, no, sir. There was not a sign. Do you think if I had known I would have let her out of my sight?"

216

He looked disgusted.

"You're a liar amongst other things. Tonight I had a telephone call from Mrs. Brown. She told me she was so worried about Mrs. Cardew that she had telephoned to you from the theatre. She told me you received her message so casually that she knew you would do nothing about it. This worried the poor old thing so that on the way home she got off her bus and went to a public call box and rang me up and begged me to come round."

Marcelle shrugged her shoulders.

"Am I to listen to talk about my mistress from all at the theatre?"

"Mrs. Brown wouldn't telephone unless it was urgent; you know that."

Marcelle shrugged again.

"I saw nothing to trouble about."

The doctor shook his head.

"You've always been a nasty bit of work, but this time you've been stupid as well. You can go to your room and pack your box. You're going to be dismissed."

Colour flared in Marcelle's cheeks.

"Oh, yes? And who are you to dismiss me? Do you pay my wages? I think when Mrs. Cardew hears how you 'ave spoken that it is more likely it is you who are dismissed; that she will get a new doctor."

"I've been trying to get Mrs. Cardew to get rid of you for ages, and I've failed, but now Mrs. Cardew has got to do what she's told. I gather from what she said before I gave her that hypodermic that she tried to injure Miss Shaw here." He raised an eyebrow at Beverley. "Is that true?"

"Yes."

"And that Annie saw what happened?"

"Yes."

He looked back to Marcelle.

"All of which proves that Mrs. Cardew must have a trustworthy maid always at hand. When she is in her present state she is not responsible for what she does. I've warned you of that, Marcelle, and told you it was your business to watch, and telephone for me. You've done neither. You've done worse; you've neglected a warning from someone else. Well, it's not going to occur again. For the present, Mrs. Cardew will have a nurse; after that I shall find her somebody. In the meantime, as I've told you, you can go. I will see that you get your notice in writing in the morning."

Marcelle's face was almost black.

"My poor mistress. It is no wonder she forget herself. You do not know what goes on in this 'ouse. That governess, she looks so good, but she is a sly one. She has stole Mr. Crewdson and so I told Mrs. Cardew tonight. Kissing be'ind doors and—"

The doctor in a step was across the room and had his hand over her mouth.

"Get out, and don't let Mr. Crewdson hear you talk like that; he mightn't be as gentle as I am."

"Oh, goodness," said Beverley, "the mess it's made, Peter and me falling in love. But none of that's true, you know."

He patted her arm.

218

"Of course I know. You and Crewdson look particularly fitted to each other. Getting married soon?"

Beverley had no time to answer for Peter came back.

"Winkle's on her way. She says we must get Scotland Yard. That Meggie has various relations she might have gone to and it'll take too long to ring them all up, not to mention it's unlikely she'd go to them."

"Oh, Miss Shaw." Annie stood in the doorway; she was still in her dressing-gown, in her hand she had some pieces of china. "She's broken her money-box. A china rabbit it was. I've found the pieces in the basket."

"How much was there in it?" asked Peter.

Annie shook her head.

"Oh, I couldn't say. They have a lot of money, don't they, Miss Shaw?"

"Mrs. Cardew gives them money whenever she feels like it," Beverley explained to the men. "I never knew how much. All the children have a lot."

"That doesn't help then." Peter walked round the room. "Beverley, you know the child better than any of us. Where would she be most likely to go? I mean, as I see the situation, she's had a fright, seeing her mother behaving like a mad woman; she's probably heard you say you are leaving and marrying me, and she knows you'll be kicked out in the morning. Now who would she turn to?"

Beverley racked her brains. Who would Meggie turn to? An idea came to her. She had made great friends with Miriam Elton. Was it possible that she had gone there? Even as hope sprang up it died. Meggie had been gone for over an hour now. If the child had money on her, it stood to reason she would have gone in a taxi, and if she had reached the vicarage it was equally certain that Sarah would have been on the telephone long ago.

"It can't be anywhere in London," she said, "because all the children are very taxi-minded. We know now that she had the money, and there is nowhere she could have got to by this time without our having heard. If she's gone to anybody it must be out of London. She would only go to someone she was fond of and—" She stopped, staring at Peter. "Oh, my goodness, one minute."

Beverley ran out of the room and up the stairs to Meggie's bedroom. She knelt down by the bed and fumbled under the mattress. In a minute she had what she wanted; Meggie's bundle of letters and photographs. It was the same rather ludicrous little bundle she had examined those weeks ago, but there was one new letter. She took it out of its envelope and with it fell a paper folder. The letter was short.

"DEAR LITTLE MEGGIE,

I am so glad you went to the Zoo with Peter again. A man like that who knows all about the animals is just the person to go with.

Thank you very much for hoping the new play will be a success, but we are not coming to London for some weeks yet. I enclose the tour card, so that you can see what a lot of places we are visiting and at your next geography lesson you can look them up.

Your affectionate friend,
GEORGE FANE."

Beverley snatched open the folder. She looked hurriedly down the list of dates. Monday, 17th April, for one week, The Pleasure Gardens, Folkestone. She pushed the letters and the photographs into a drawer, and ran downstairs back to the drawing-room. Winkle had arrived in her absence, but she paid no attention to her, nor to Annie, nor to the doctor; she looked directly at Peter.

"He's at the Pleasure Gardens Theatre, Folkestone, this week. I must go there at once."

The night porter knocked on George Fane's door. George rolled over in his sleep and opened one eye. He glared angrily at the luminous figures on his bedside clock. Half-past four!

"Come in. What on earth is it? Is the house on fire?"

The hall porter was as shocked as George to find himself disturbing a visitor at such an hour.

"No, sir. But there's a young lady to see you, sir. You could have knocked me down with a feather, sir. I was just giving the final cleaning to my hall, as it's part of my work to brush it of a night-time, when in she comes, sir. Came all the way in a taxi from London."

"A young lady!" George, looking horrified, got out of bed and put on his dressing-gown. His still drowsy mind roved frantically through his women friends.

"What does she look like? She's not got platinum hair and an American accent, has she? If she has, I'm not going to see her, and you can tell her from me I'm not being had for that kind of mug."

"Oh, no, sir." The porter looked shocked. "I shouldn't

have said young lady, sir, she's a child."

"A child! Good God!"

"Yes, sir," said the porter. "Very independent young lady, sir. Very royal in her way, in a manner of speaking. Wearing white fur, sir—ermine I think it is."

"Oh, well." George rummaged for his bedroom slippers. "I'd better go and see, I suppose."

Meggie was sitting on the circular seat surrounding a group of ferns in the middle of the hall. George saw who it was as he stepped out of the lift.

"Meggie! What on earth?"

Meggie got up. If he had known more about children he would have noticed how appallingly white she was, and the nervous grip of her hands as she held on to his.

"I've run away," she explained. "I heard things so I know I can't go home any more, and Miss Shaw, that's our governess, is going to marry Peter, and so I came here."

"But why here?"

Meggie was surprised at that question.

"But of course I came here. You see, now that my governess is going to marry Peter, and they are both going to Kenya, you are the only real friend I've got."

George liked children in their proper places. He liked children that he could spoil in tea shops, giving them far too many cream buns, or to take to the Zoo, and to Madame Tussaud's, to matinées of such plays as *Where the Rainbow Ends*, but he did not like children at half-past four in the morning, and certainly not children who said they'd run away from home and had come to him because they said he was the only friend they'd got. He looked at Meggie severely.

"You're a very naughty girl. I haven't the faintest idea what to do with you." He turned to the hall porter who had been listening sympathetically to the conversation. "Is there a housekeeper who could look after her until I can make arrangements for sending her back?"

"Back!" gasped Meggie. "But I'm never going back. I'll kill myself first. You don't know what happened last night."

"Do stop talking rot. Of course I don't know what happened last night, because I wasn't there. Whatever it was it can't be so very terrible; just keep quiet while I make arrangements. What's your telephone number? I must ring your people."

"If you ring them up or try and send me back, I'll throw myself into the sea."

"Do talk sense," said George, exasperated. "What did you suppose I was going to do with you?"

"I thought you'd let me stay with you. You've always said we were friends and friends help each other."

"Now get it into your head once and for all, my girl, that you're going right back where you belong, and you're not going to jump into any sea because the housekeeper will look after you."

Meggie stared at him, two tears trickling down her cheeks.

"Everybody's the same," she said in a whisper. "They like you a little while, and then they go away, or else they just stop liking you. I wish I was dead."

"If you ask me," said the hall porter, "the young lady

would be the better for a glass of milk. I'll just slip along to the kitchen."

"Well, don't be long," said George, nervous of being left alone with Meggie.

The porter smiled at Meggie.

"Would you fancy a biscuit? We've some nice *petit beurre,* or perhaps I could find some with sugar on."

"I wish I was dead," Meggie whispered again. She leant limply against the door of the lift.

George looked at her anxiously, suddenly noticing her colour.

"You look awfully queer. You don't feel sick, do you?"

"Things are going round a bit," Meggie murmured.

The hall porter, who had children of his own, picked Meggie up in his arms.

"Milk with a drop of brandy in it is what she needs. Put some cushions on that sofa, sir. She's come all over alike. No wonder, taxi all the way from London."

Meggie, lying flat, felt better physically and so able to realize more clearly the full horror of what had happened. With violent imagination she had built on to George's hearty friendliness an entirely mythical belief in his friendship and understanding. In the horror of seeing her mother's feet turn utterly to clay, and the confusion of hearing that Beverley was going, she had felt for a few moments as if her world were toppling round her, then out of the ruins just one figure emerged—George. He would understand. From that thought to dressing, to smashing her moneybox, to collecting her money, to running out into the road and getting a taxi had been practically one action. She knew George was at Folkestone. Her theatrical knowledge told her that an actor of his standing would be living in one of the best hotels and should not be difficult to find.

The taxi driver had been the first difficulty. He had been all for thinking the police station was a better place to take her to than Folkestone, but Meggie's histrionic ability had come to her rescue. The story of the surprise she was giving her mother when she met her by the boat train in the morning, together with five pounds in miscellaneous notes and silver, won him over. Once inside the hotel she had relaxed, a little of the terror of the night had receded. George was here. George would understand. George would make everything feel better. But now George had let her down, or rather not so much let her down as opened her eyes. There never had been a George, at least not the George she had seen. Sipping the hot milk and brandy provided by the porter, Meggie's self-control went hopelessly. At first it was tears that dripped down her cheeks, then it was loud sobbing.

"Oh, my, sir," said the porter, "stop her, do. You'll have all the guests awake."

But George could only glare at Meggie, and make hissing noises as he would make to a horse.

"There, there, old girl; pull up, old girl, do. Whoa, old girl." He turned to the porter. "For goodness' sake get that housekeeper."

The porter looked doubtful.

"She's a very severe lady, Mrs. Meadows, sir, not one to comfort a young lady in her state."

"Whoa, there, whoa, old girl." George patted Meggie fervently on the shoulder and looked desperately at the porter over his shoulder. "I don't care what the old hag looks like as long as she can take charge of her."

The porter, shaking his head very doubtfully both on Meggie's behalf and on his own, as he knew what Mrs. Meadows would be like roused at five in the morning, disappeared towards the servants' quarters, and at that moment George remembered the telephone. He went over to the porter's desk and took down both halves of the London telephone directory. He scratched his head and stared at them, while he wondered would the kid's mother be under D for Dale, or C for Cardew; anyway, they were both in the same half. With his back to Meggie he pushed the red book out of his way, opened the blue book and turned the pages to the CAR'S.

Meggie was so far gone in her hysteria that she really could scarcely hear what was said to her. But it so happened that George was in her line of vision, and she saw him push aside the red telephone book, and some part of her brain that was still under control recorded what he was going to do. She could not stop herself from crying, but she stuffed a corner of her coat into her mouth, slipped off the sofa, and crept out of the hotel.

The porter and George both lost their heads when they found Meggie had gone. George told the porter that he was a damned fool, that the girl couldn't have gone, she had never left the hall, and the porter pointing to the sofa said lugubriously: "And if 'er body's found at the bottom of the cliffs in the morning, you'll he to blame, sir."

It was at this moment that Beverley and Peter arrived.

George was so thoroughly shocked and depressed by all that had happened that he had to start at the wrong end of the story.

"If she got out it was like magic; one moment she was lying on the sofa, and the next not a sight of her."

Beverley's face, which was pale and drawn enough already, turned paler. She took hold of George by his dressing-gown and gave him a shake.

"You mean she's been here, and you let her go?"

"We didn't let her go," George expostulated. "I was just ringing up her mother, and the porter here was getting the housekeeper to look after her. We couldn't let her go, she said she'd throw herself into the sea."

"What!" Peter looked round at the porter. "How long ago was this?"

"Not more than a minute before you came, sir."

Peter made for the door.

"Quick, then, all of you, she can't be far."

It was Beverley who found Meggie. The child had run down one of the cliff paths towards the sea. In spite of faintness she had gone quickly; she was on the beach when Beverley found her. What she might have done, or had planned to do, Beverley did not know. By the time she came on her, emotion had been too much for her. She was collapsed in a heap. Beverley knelt by her and put her arms round her, managing somehow to keep her relief out of her voice.

"Good gracious me, Meggie, what are you doing down here?"

Meggie shook her head vaguely.

"I feel terribly sick, Shawskins."

"And no wonder," said Beverley. "Running about like this all night. Never mind, we'll soon have you better. I'll get the hall porter and Peter to carry you somewhere where we can get a taxi to take you back to the hotel."

Meggie clutched her.

"I can't stop in that hotel; he doesn't want me."

Beverley squeezed her closer.

"Well, he must have been rather surprised at you turning up like that. You can't blame him."

A wave of sickness surged over Meggie; she closed her eyes. When she was better she looked up.

"Where shall I go, Shawskins? I can't go home. You do see that, don't you?"

"We needn't discuss that now, need we?" Beverley suggested gently. "You're going to bed for a bit, anyway, before we think of you going anywhere."

Meggie shook her head. Her mouth set in lines of grim determination.

"I'm not going home. I'm frightened, and you won't be there."

Beverley thought of Doctor Grey. He had made it clear that he considered that one way and another, they had the whip hand over Margot. She took a risk.

"I'm coming with you."

"But Mummy said—"

Beverley managed to laugh.

"Your mother was ill, she didn't mean a word of it."

"And aren't you going to marry Peter?"

Tenderness swept over Beverley.

"Of course I am, but not till I've found the right person to come and look after you."

"There couldn't be anybody else I'd like."

Beverley saw Peter running up the promenade and called out to him, then she turned back to Meggie.

"There are plenty of people. I shall find one that you'll like awfully, and I shan't leave until I've found her."

Another wave of sickness and faintness overcame Meggie.

"Promise?" she asked faintly.

Beverley stroked the hair off the child's forehead.

"I promise."

CHAPTER THIRTEEN

BEVERLEY and Peter sat under a tree in the Green Park. They had turned their chairs to face the tree because Beverley was crying and she did not want the passers-by to see.

"That seems to be all there is to say about it," said Peter in a bitter voice. "If you prefer someone else's children to marrying me, it's no good my arguing."

"But I don't. I want to marry you more than anything else in the world, and you know it. But you must see that I can't leave them just now."

"I don't see. I suppose they could get another governess, couldn't they? You aren't the only one in the world."

"You don't know what the house has been like these last three weeks. The doctor's allowing Mrs. Cardew to rehearse again now, but she's got a nurse, you know, and she's not allowed to go near the schoolroom at all, or to see anybody when she comes back from the theatre. Meggie is getting worse from not seeing her mother. She keeps remembering her the last time she saw her, and it's becoming a positive phobia that she never wants to see her again."

"I'm sorry about Meggie, but I cannot see why our lives have got to be ruined for somebody else's child."

"No, I know you can't." Beverley choked back a sob. "Meggie's so pathetic. She's in an awful state of nerves, and it's taken the form of her not bearing me out of her sight. After all, a year isn't long, and I'll be waiting for you when you come back."

Peter leant over and gripped her hands.

"I hate to say this, Beverley, but that's no good to me. I want all your love. And I can't have got it; if I had you'd come with me now."

Beverley forced back a sob.

"You're muddling two things. I think these children are my duty."

He got up.

"We've talked round and round this subject and we're getting nowhere. This is good-bye."

"Peter!" Beverley gripped him. "You can't go like that. In a year we'll feel just the same."

"Perhaps." It was all he could do not to take her in his arms. "But I'm a primitive person. A lot of my time has been spent in forests and wild lands. I know when two creatures love each other they must allow nothing and nobody to keep them apart." He gave her arm a squeeze. "Good-bye."

Beverley got up. She made a step to run after him, but she held herself back.

"Peter!" she called, but her voice was a whisper. Then as she saw him walking rapidly away from her, she put her hands over her mouth and shook with silent sobs.

Beverley had sent the children out with Annie and she hoped to sneak into the house unobserved, but Winkle was in the hall. Winkle gave her a startled look and then took hold of her arm.

"Come into my room and have some tea, dear."

Beverley was too wretched to know or care what she did. Quite unresisting she was led into Winkle's study and pushed into an armchair. Winkle pretended to be busy with some papers and said nothing at all, until the tea tray arrived, and she had poured Beverley out a cup and put it beside her. "Drink that down." Beverley, obediently as a child, sipped her tea. "You look quite worn out. I was wanting to see you, dear. I thought as we hadn't fixed a governess, it would make it easier for the children if they were sent to their grandmother for a week or two. Annie can go with them, and it won't hurt them to miss their lessons for a little. I'm sure I can find a nice governess before they come back."

Beverley put down her cup.

"There's no need. I'm staying on."

Winkle took a deep breath. Through these last weeks she had been afraid to hear just that statement. Each time the question of interviewing governesses had turned up, Beverley had shelved it.

"You can't do that. You mustn't do that. Apart from anything else, Mrs. Cardew wouldn't hear of it."

Beverley leant over for her bag and took out a letter.

"I wrote to Mrs. Cardew. Here's her answer."

Winkle took the letter.

"DEAR MISS SHAW,

Very well. I understand from my doctor that he considers that for the moment, at any rate, the schoolroom is better left in your charge, and I personally consider that your marriage to Mr.

232

Crewdson would have been a great mistake. He is not of your world. Later on, when I am in better health, I shall make entirely different arrangements for my children, but for the moment, provided I do not have to see you, you can remain in the house.

Yours sincerely,
MARGOT CARDEW."

Winkle folded the letter and put it back in its envelope. "It's not my place to advise you, but—"

Beverley gave her a watery smile

"I know all the things you're going to say, but my mind's made up. I think that all this upset was my fault. After all, I knew how Mrs. Cardew felt about Peter. I'd no right to have let it happen, or rather when I knew it was happening I should have given in my notice and gone at once. It's quite all right, I've seen him and everything's over." She got up. "If you don't mind I'll go to my room."

Winkle sat at her desk and stared into space. She was not seeing her little office at number ten Way Street, but an overcrowded, small sitting-room at Wimbledon. It was wartime. Eddie, in khaki, was going down the little path that led to the gate. She remembered how odd and blurred he had looked through her tears, and how she had moved aside the Nottingham lace curtains to try and get him in better focus. She remembered the door opening and her mother coming in. How she had brushed away her tears, and patted and settled her mother on the sofa. How her mother had said: "Was that Eddie who just went out?" in the rather hurt, fretful voice she used when she spoke of him. How she had stooped down and kissed her, and said, "Yes, but he's not coming back. I've just been telling him that I didn't think I could leave you, that you and I have always been so dependent on each other," and how her mother had said, "That's my good girl. I don't mind being left, dear, but I never really cared for Eddie, and I'm sure the marriage would have been a mistake."

Winkle blinked to clear the vision of that little scene. Suddenly, with grim determination, she got up. She took her coat, gloves, bag and hat from the cupboard. She pulled her coat on and with scarcely a glance in the glass jammed on her hat. "It's not going to happen if I can prevent it," she told the room fiercely, and went out.

Sarah was with the children when Winkle was announced. She had, of course, heard of her from Beverley, so she put the children in charge of Miriam and hurried downstairs.

"You don't know me, Miss Cox," said Winkle nervously. "But I've heard so much of you, and I know you're a good friend of Beverley Shaw's. She's broken off her engagement. She mustn't be allowed to do it. I did it myself once and I know the unhappiness it causes."

Sarah pointed to the sofa.

"Do sit down and tell me all about it."

In a twittering, nervous way, Winkle described all that had happened in the last three weeks—Meggie's state of mind, and Beverley's reaction. At the end, Sarah looked at her squarely.

"What do you want me to do about it?"

"Well, my dear, you are, I know, leaving here in a few

months. Of course, I'm taking a great deal upon myself, but I was wondering—You see, Mrs. Cardew is not allowed to see the children, and the whole management of the house is in my hands, in conjunction with Doctor Grey, of course. Of course, I don't know how your employers would consider this suggestion, but I thought perhaps, a little house, somewhere nice, like Seaford. Quiet, you know, with no vulgar people about. Of course, I know there are three children here, and our three, and that makes rather a lot, especially with Betsy so difficult, but I would, of course, send Annie with you, and the nicest of the maids who could be spared."

Sarah laid her hand on Winkle's knee.

"Do let me get this clear, Miss Winks. Are you suggesting that I take Beverley's place?"

"Well, yes, dear. Of course, it would be ideal, but I know you can't just now, so I thought that if they could all go away together, and really Seaford's very healthy and very quiet. You can tell Mr. Elton that, because I know the clergy are particular."

Sarah, in a burst of enthusiasm, put an arm round Winkle.

"But it's a most gorgeous idea. The children are looking peaky, and Seaford would do them marvels of good. Do you think Beverley would agree?"

Winkle shook her head.

"I doubt it. She feels terribly to blame for everything that's happened. No, dear, what I think is that the idea must come from Meggie. Could you come back with me now and see her?"

"Now look, dear," said Winkle as the taxi stopped at number ten Way Street, "you go and sit in my little study and I shall send Meggie down there; it may not be easy, because, of course, Miss Shaw must not know."

"What do you want me for, Winkle?" said Meggie as she came down the stairs by Winkle's side.

"It's Miss Cox, dear; she's got a little plan to discuss with you. Run along, dear, she's waiting for you in my study."

Sarah kissed Meggie and drew her on to the sofa beside her.

"How are you, darling? Miriam sends her love."

"I'm all right."

Sarah felt that Meggie was nervous. She broke into what she had to say at once.

"Look here, old lady, did you know Beverley Shaw has decided not to marry Peter Crewdson?"

Meggie nodded.

"She's just told me."

"Did she tell you why?"

"Yes. She said she'd found out that she'd rather stop with us."

Sarah looked her straight in the eyes.

"Did you believe her?"

Meggie wriggled uncomfortably.

"She's very fond of us." Her voice was truculent.

Sarah nodded.

"That's perfectly true; but the real reason she's not marrying him is you, Meggie. She knows you are going to miss her, and she's sorry for you."

Meggie looked at her hands.

"She's promised to stay."

"You're very fond of her, aren't you? Are you fond enough of her to do something great for her?"

"I don't want her to go away," said Meggie stubbornly.

"Not even if you knew that it was making her desperately unhappy to stop here."

Meggie's eyes filled with tears; she looked up at Sarah.

"I know she's miserable; her face is miserable, but I'm frightened without her. We haven't anybody else."

Sarah put her arm round her.

"I know I'm a poor substitute, but would you be frightened with me?"

Meggie looked puzzled.

"But you've got the Eltons?"

"Just now, but Winkle has an idea that I might take you all, the Eltons and yourselves, to the sea somewhere, and by the time we come back, Mrs. Elton will be better, and I could come and look after you."

Meggie clasped and unclasped her hands.

"I do like you awfully, Coxy, but—"

"She's terribly unhappy," said Sarah. "Suppose you came with me now and we went and saw Mr. Crewdson. Suppose you brought him back to her. It would be doing a great thing for a friend."

The colour came and went in Meggie's face. Twice she opened her mouth to speak, twice she changed her mind. Then she got up.

"Wait here. I'll go and get my coat."

Beverley was kissing Betsy and David good night when

237

Meggie came to fetch her.

"Could you come here a minute, Shawskins?"

Beverley came out into the passage.

"Where have you and Winkle been?" For all her effort her voice was dull and lifeless.

"It was a secret. Something I wanted to do for you." She drew Beverley up the passage towards the nursery. "There's somebody waiting for you in there."

Beverley looked down at her.

"You mean Peter?" In spite of herself her voice throbbed on the word.

Meggie nodded.

"Yes. I've told him everything. He'll tell you." She flung her arms round Beverley. "And please it's because I love you."

Peter strode across the room and took Beverley in his arms.

"I called you," he said, kissing every bit of her face as he spoke, "Joan of Arc, the first time I saw you. You looked so gallant and purposeful. But I thought today in my masculine pride that even your sense of duty would break down, when it came to us losing each other. But I hear from Meggie I was wrong. You are unshakable. It's taken the combined ingenuity of Winkle and Miss Cox and the unselfishness of Meggie to find our way out."

"But—"

"Now listen."

Beverley leant against him and heard what had been planned. Her heart was singing and her eyes shining when he had finished.

"Oh, Peter, and I thought I'd lost you."

There was a long silence while he kissed her. Then he said:

"All this has made me hungry. Let's go out to dinner."

"But—"

He put his hand over her mouth.

"Let me finish. And we'll invite Meggie to come with us."

Other books by
SUSAN SCARLETT

published by
Greyladies

SUMMER PUDDING

Take one farm in wartime England, a motherless young girl and her father. Add a young woman bombed out of her London office, a beautiful but selfish younger sister, a sick mother, a resentful housekeeper, a retired colonel and his daughter at the Big House, and a canny old codger too old for the army. Mix well and leave to simmer for a delicious frothy summer confection.

Originally published in 1943.

PETER AND PAUL

Twins Petronella and Pauline (Peter and Paul) leave their country vicarage home to work at 'Reboux', a fashionable London dress shop.

Stunningly beautiful Peter inspires owner David Bliss's best designs, while kind Paul becomes friend and confidante to the rest of the staff.

One twin loves David but he is smitten with the other – but does either of them stand a chance against the ruthless and manipulative Moira, who wants David for herself?

A charming love story, originally published as a magazine serial in 1939.

LOVE IN A MIST

When four year old Paul, already somewhat pampered and spoilt, is chosen for a part in a film his unexpected good fortune triggers major family ructions. It takes all matriarch Emma Tring's subtle diplomacy not just to avoid discord but to bring her unsettled family closer together. A theatrical theme spiced with family in-fighting, difficult children, a wiser older woman: this is what this author does best. Noel Streatfeild spent some time in Hollywood researching the film background for her children's novel *The Painted Garden,* research which also ensures an utterly believable background for the Rose of England film studios in *Love in a Mist.*

PIROUETTE

Ballet Shoes was never like this! Young Judith Nell is torn between the demanding discipline of the ballet and the love of a good man. The single-minded ruthlessness of Russian emigrée Madame Tania, coupled with an equally single-minded Ballet Mother who never wavers from her ambition for her daughter, don't leave Judith any time for anything else – until Paul Conquest falls in love with her. Will she allow Madame and Mummy to make all her decisions for her? It's time for her to grow up and take charge of her own life.

CLOTHES-PEGS

Promoted from humble seamstress to glamorous model in a top London fashion store, Annabel is transported to a world of cocktails, luxurious cars, Elizabethan mansions – and back-biting jealousy.

Miss Streatfeild, who did her own stint as a mannequin, presents a convincing behind-the-scenes picture of exhaustion, boredom, enforced camaraderie and wonderfully acerbic bitchiness. Sustained by glasses of port and bromo-seltzers, the girls are on the edge of Society; still regarded as the equivalent of chorus-girls, they are good for a dinner-date or weekend rendezvous but not for marriage.

Annabel comes from a happy, down-to-earth and hard-working family, brought up by the eminently wise Ethel to know right from wrong. So can her romance with a Lord really be doomed?